Ellice Hopkins

Autumn Swallows

A Book of Lyrics

Ellice Hopkins

Autumn Swallows
A Book of Lyrics

ISBN/EAN: 9783744787802

Printed in Europe, USA, Canada, Australia, Japan

Cover: Foto ©Andreas Hilbeck / pixelio.de

More available books at **www.hansebooks.com**

A Book of Lyrics

AUTUMN SWALLOWS

A BOOK OF LYRICS

BY

ELLICE HOPKINS

London

MACMILLAN AND CO.

1883

LONDON : PRINTED BY
SPOTTISWOODE AND CO., NEW-STREET SQUARE
AND PARLIAMENT STREET

CONTENTS.

CONTENTS.

SONNETS.

LIFE IN DEATH.

I HEARD him in the autumn winds,
    I felt him in the cadent star,
And in the shattered mirror of the wave,
    That still in death a rapture finds,
    I caught his image faint and far;
And musing in the twilight on the grave,
    I heard his footstep stealing by,
    Where the long churchyard grasses sigh.

    But never might I see his face,
    Though everywhere I found Death's hand,
And his large language all things living spake;
    And ever heavy with the grace

B

Of bygone things through all the land
The song of birds or distant church-bells brake.
   ' I will arise and seek his face,'
   I said, ' ere wrapped in his embrace.'

   ' For Death is king of life,' I cried,
   ' Beauty is but his pomp and state ;
His kiss is on the apple's crimson cheek,
   And with the grape his feet are dyed,
   Treading at noon the purple vat ;
And flowers, more radiant hued, more quickly seek
   His face, betraying, in disguise
   Their young blooms are but autumn dyes.'

   Then I arose ere dawn, and found
   A faded lily.   ' Lo, 'tis He !
I will surprise him in his golden bed,
   Where, muffled close from light and sound,
   He sleeps the day up.'   Noiselessly
I drew the faded curtains from his head,
   And, peeping, found, not Death below,
   But fairy life set all arow.

A chrysalis next I chanced upon :
'Death in this dusty shroud has dwelt ! '
But stooping saw a wingèd Thing, sun-kist,
Crusted with jewels Life had won
From Death's dim dust ; and as I knelt,
Some passion shook the jewels into mist,
Some ecstasy of coming flight,
And lo, he passed in morning light.

And as I paced, still questioning,
Behold, a dead bird at my feet ;
The faded violets of his filmy eyes,
And tender loosened throat, to sing
No more to us his nocturns sweet,
Told me that death at length before me lies.
But gazing, quick I turned in fear,
Not Death, but teeming Life was there.

Then haply Death keeps house within ?
And with the scalpel of keen thought
I traced the chemic travail of the brain,
The throb and pulse of Life's machine,

And mystic force with force still caught
In the embrace that maketh one of twain ;
     And all the beatings, swift and slow,
     Of Life's vibration to and fro.

     And still I found the downward swing,
     Decay, but ere I cried ' Lo, here ! '
The upward stroke rang out glad life and breath ;
     And still dead winters changed with spring,
     And graves the new birth's cradle were ;
And still I grasped the flying skirts of Death,
     And still he turned, and, beaming fair,
     The radiant face of Life was there !

THE GOLDEN LADDER.

WHEN torn with Passion's insecure delights,
    By Love's dear torment, ceaseless changes worn,
As my swift sphere full twenty days and nights
    Did make ere one slow morn and eve were born ;

I passed within the dim sweet world of flowers,
    Where only harmless lights, not hearts, are broken,
And weep but the sweet-watered summer showers—
    World of white joys, cool dews, and peace unspoken ;

I started even there among the flowers,
    To find the tokens mute of what I fled,
Passions, and forces, and resistless powers,
    That have uptorn the world, and stirred the dead.

In secret bowers of amethyst and rose,
   Close wrapped in fragrant golden curtains laid,
Where silver lattices to morn unclose,
   The fairy lover clasps his flower-maid.

Patient she yields to his caresses' strength,
   And in her simple bosom 'neath fair skies
Love's sweetness bears, till, giving birth at length,
   She shuts her tender lids, and sweetly dies.

Ye blessed children of the jocund day !
   What mean these mysteries of love and birth ?
Caught up like solemn words by babes at play,
   Who know not what they babble in their mirth.

Or of one stuff has some Hand made us all,
   Baptised us all in one great sequent plan,
Where deep to ever vaster deep may call,
   And all their large expression find in man ?

Flowers climb to birds, and birds and beasts to man,
   And man to God, by some strong instinct driven ;

And so the golden ladder upward ran,
  Its foot among the flowers, its top in heaven.

All lives man lives ; of matter first, then tends
  To plants, an animal next unconscious, dim,
A man, a spirit last, the cycle ends,
  That all creation weds with God in him.

And if he fall, a world in him doth fall,
  All things decline to lower uses ; while
The golden chain that bound the each to all,
  Falls broken in the dust, a linkless pile.

And Love's fair sacraments and mystic rite
  In Nature, that their consummation find
In wedded hearts, and union infinite
  With the divine, of married mind with mind,

Foul symbols of an idol temple grow,
  And sun-white Love is blackened into lust,
And man's impure doth into flower-cups flow,
  And the fair Kosmos mourneth in the dust.

O Thou, out-topping all we know or think,
   Far off yet nigh, out-reaching all we see,
Hold Thou my hand, that so the topmost link
   Of the great chain may hold, from us to Thee ;

And from my heaven-touched life may downward flow
   Prophetic promise of a grace to be ;
And flower, and bird, and beast, may upward grow,
   And find their highest linked to God in me.

THE MOONLIGHT PATH.

BY THE SEA.

Up to these darkling, faltering feet
Yon path of tremulous splendour comes
Apocalyptic, golden, sweet.

Across the deep those splendours wend,
The deep that I must tread alone,
Nor know its rise, nor know its end.

No mortal path, but mystic, strange,
I seek it not, it seeketh me;
It follows me where'er I range.

Its secret light I only see,
To far-off eyes it seemeth dark ;
This glory was but born with me.

In gloom I seek an unknown strand,
My onward step is washed with fire,
The fire of God that leads to land.

Out of the fathomless gloom I hear
The voices of a world in pain,
Filling the vacant atmosphere.

Infinite murmurs of despair,
Clap of aërial hands, faint sighs,
Sobbings and plaints and moaning prayer.

‘ Is there no light for these ? ’ I cry ;
‘ This narrow path suffices not ;
Light for my loved, or else I die ! ’

In vain !   Between two nights I tread
The lane of light, Thy feet, O Christ,
Walking the sea across it shed.

‘ Then hither, share this radiance sweet ;
The growing shadow of the wave
Here breaks in splendour at your feet.’

'Nay, where thou art but gloom we mark ;
And if perchance we loose thy hand,
We fear to falter in the dark.'

'Ah me ! Ah me ! Ye say but true ;
This path, that broadens to the verge,
Here is not wide enough for two.'

Out of the fathomless gloom again
Sweeps o'er bowed head and darkened heart
The voices of a world in pain.

Infinite wailings of despair,
Clap of aërial hands, low moans,
Sobbings and plaints and fruitless prayer.

'Is there no light, no hope for these ?
Must I walk lonely in the light,
And these be lost on darkened seas ? '

Then like a long low beam of light,
That makes the chilliest fog-drop burn,
A voice came falling through the night :

No soul is born, no eye looks forth,
But with it born this path of light,
Its splendid heritage from birth.

The darkest feet that saddest wend,
By this long charity of light,
Are golden-linked to God our end.

To thee 'tis dark where'er thou roam,
But each this hidden radiance knows,
That sweet, persistent, calls him home.

Ah, look ! this deep, where shadows meet,
Is crossed by myriad tracks of fire,
Bright beckoning hands and gleaming feet.

Nor only so, ah, narrow heart !
Couldst thou but broaden out thy gaze,
Bid thy mortality depart,

Then, swept on thy enraptured soul,
Yon sea would into splendour burst,
Baptised in light from pole to pole.

THE EAGLE.

BEHOLD, an eagle awaking to jubilant life
In the mighty prime of a young creation's morn,
Awaking to life upon a stupendous crag
Of some limitless lone Australasian continent.
Lo, as he opens his blue-filmed eyes on the sun,
From the shadowless height of the granite beaten with
     noon,
Unknowing of aught but the callow life in his veins,
Can he know what it is, that burning pain of the light,
Strong pain that quivers and flashes through all his
     nerves ?
Nought knows he of eagle vision fed on the light ;
Nought of the bounteous wideflowing garb of the day,
As knotted in fire, divine insupportable fire,
Ever it hangs round the mighty shoulders of Him,

The immutable Angel of thunder, of change, of the
    world,
Immutable though his swift sphere still change to his
    touch ;
Nought would he know but pain, unquenchable pain.
Yea, though unblenching he gazed with quivering
    nerves,
Striving to pierce the unknown heart of the wonder,
The inscrutable cause of all his ceaseless distress,
Would not the answer remorseless come back still as
    pain,
Pain pealed back from the heart of the pitiless glory,
Pain of ineffable light that smites into darkness ?

O man ! O humanity ! O thou my brother !
Made with thy soul to mirror the infinite light,
Creature of God, of a day, outlived by the fragilest
    flower,
Converging the limitless ocean of light to a point !
Canst thou put on the glory of all that is,
And not quiver, not faint, not know it as infinite
    pain ?

As wrong, as failure, as death, as ceasing to be,

Which yet is the unexprest glory, the wonder that is,

This vesture of large-limbed Gods that o'erwhelmeth
thee,

Falling in folds majestic of sunset and dawn

About thy death agony, mocked with ironical beams.

Yea, they who after long searchings have found her at
length,

Glory's ineffable self, the Unspeakable,

Dizzied and maddened by her insupportable light,

Have fallen down blind in the dark of the blaze at
her feet,

Crying, 'We know not, yea, and never can know.'

Ah, pitiful eyelids ! creeds of mankind ! dear white
faiths !

Too soon, ah, too soon have we parted with you, too
soon

Have lifted our eyes to That no man may behold

And live, but his heart is rent and shattered by
lightning.

Drop pitiful, healing, again o'er our strained eyes,

Let in the light in soft dreams and visions of night,

Fleeting forms that embody for us the immutable
>   truth ;

Till in the eagle flight of our deathless course,

We are able to bear the awful light of what is.

A PORTRAIT.

To S. A.

A FACE I met among a London crowd,

That present, yet seemed absent, with a light

Of other worlds slow breaking through the eyes

When for a moment's space he looked our way ;

Pale-hued as frescoes faded with the sun,

The high bald brows with a dark skull-cap crowned,

A face I knew was strange yet seen before.

And through the idle buzz of this and that,

I moved perplexed among a phantom crowd,

Dim glimmerings of old-world consciousness,

And strange weird visitings of former states,

That lie below the deep-sea springs of thought ;

Forgotten things still aching to be known,

Like drownèd cities wavering up confused

With sea-bent beams.   Until at length some door,

Touched by a groping hand all unawares,
Flew open, and let in upon the will
The long-forgotten thing I vainly sought.

.   .   .   .   .

Far hence, high up among the Southern Alps,
A little chapel with its dead is seen,
Set in the lonely stillness of the hills,
Most like a mother keeping watch beside
Her sleeping children with unsleeping love.
The mountain pastures fair come rippling down
About its crumbling walls, and on the graves
Break soft in rainbow-tinted foam, and crown
The fading memories with fadeless flowers,
Making death beautiful with life.   Hard by
A brook brings down the freshness of the hills,
Flinging its silver fringes o'er the stones
In wayward ecstasies of hill-born joy,
And makes the silence audible about it.
And all the place is sweet with sun warmed pines,
Their sun-struck pillars keen against the dark
Of woven boughs, and all the valley side
Seen purpling through them into mountain bloom.

And to its lowly door a little path
Comes swerving up through bruisèd hillside balms,
Trodden by meek and weary men and women,
That hither come to lean their tired hearts
Against the Eternal Love, and patient rest
A little at His feet.

        A humble place
Unvisited, and by the world unknown,
Yet on its whitewashed walls some hand of old—
Haply the angel-monk's within whose dim
And cloistered thoughts God and His saints still
      walked
In glory up and down—had painted there
The Master teaching, and a sunburnt group
Of peasants listening to His words intent
With level gaze, while from the calm sad brow
And calmly parted lips calm wisdom flowed,
Washing life clear, touching its tangled chords,
Misknown till came the Hand that strung their fires,
To Heaven. sent airs.   And all the mountain side
Seems listening with the group entrancèd there ;
Listen the solemn upward-pointing pines ;

Listen the lizards basking on the wall's

Hot, sun-bleached stones ; listen the mountain
   flowers,

With the sweet, dim, uncomprehending looks

Of little children sitting hushed and still

In consecrated places.   Listening ever

They stand, those silent shadows on the wall,

When the East window drinks the first grey light,

To when the setting sun incarnadines

His slanted spear within a martyr's heart ;

While men and women idly pass and go

Like phantoms round them, till they seem the real,

Clothed on with the immutability

Of the eternal hills, and all things else

But passing shows.

        But on the right of them,

Skirting the group, an empty space is seen.

Still to this day the simple peasants say,

One night the storm was loud upon the hills,

And the wet pine-boughs swashed against the panes,

The rain broke in and wrought that vacant place ;

But now I know thy face, thy form was there

I met by chance among the London crowd ;
Nor wholly yet the listening look intent
Had died from out of thy mild eyes, the head
A little forward bent as though to catch
Some fading breath of far-off harmonies
Our duller sense was all too gross to hear.

Ah, wherefore didst thou leave the listening group
With Christ and beauty on the mountain side ?
Leave the cool silence of the morning skies,
And evening wells of gold in herby hollows,
Where the blue shadows lengthening love to linger ;
And all the flowery sun-slopes lifted joy,
To mingle with the loud distressful roar
Of human life that thunders through our streets,
Or wake at night to the uneasy silence
Of the great city in its broken sleep,—
Silence that is not silence to the heart,
But unheard groans and wailings of despair ;
Haunting the harsh discordant ways of men,
Beset with ills not thine the force to stem
That drown the finer voices of thy soul

And leave thee orphaned of melodious joys,
Till thou a vexèd shadow among men
Dost grow and fade perceptibly away
From all that is to that which only seems.

Ah, yet methinks, ere that may be, ere yet
Beneath our worldling touch thy wings are bruised,
And all thy strange, unearthly beauty slain,
Our wrangling marts will know that still lit face
No more ; but thou wilt upward flit from us,
And silently resume thine olden place,
Still kept for thee among the listening group ;
And as a great grave eagle spreads his wings
For flight, and springing upwards to the light,
The huge world reels away from him, and swoons
With all its lessening cities into mist,
So all the sounding nothingness of men
Will fade and die from off thy listening soul,
And leave thee standing face to face with Truth.

BORMUS.[1]

A LINUS SONG.

. . . . λίνον δ' ὑπὸ καλὸν ἄειδε
Λεπταλέῃ φωνῇ.—*Il.* xviii. 571.

Down from the lifted cornfield trips
The child with ripe red-berried lips,
The radiant mountain boy with eyes
   Blue as wet gentians in the shade,
His golden hair all wet with heat,
   Limp as the meadow-gold new laid ;
And as a russet fir-cone brown,
   An earthen pitcher gaily swings
Upon his little shoulder borne,
   Water to fetch from sunless springs ;
And while the flowers his bare feet brush
Loud sings he like a mountain thrush.

[1] See Note 1 at the end of the book.

Ah cornflowers blue and poppies red,
Weep, for our little Love is dead.

By paths that through sweet hay new mown
Like hillside brooks come leaping down,
Past silver slabs of morning, where
    The wet crags flash the sunlight back,
Past the warm runnels in the grass,
    Whose course the purple orchids track,
And down the shining upland slopes,
    And herby dells all dark with pine,
Incarnate gladness, leaps the child,
    Still singing like a bird divine,
His little pattering sunburnt feet
With bruisèd meadow spikenard sweet.

Ah cornflowers blue and poppies red,
Weep, for our little Love is dead.

Too soon, ah me, too bitter soon
He reached the dell unsunned at noon,

Where in long flutes the water falls
   Into a deep and glimmering pool,
And struck from out the dripping rocks
   The silver water sparks all cool
Spangle the chilly cavern-dark,
   And clear-cut ferns green fringe the gloom,
And with continuous sound the air
   Trembles, and all the still perfume,—
Here came the child for water chill,
The sultry reapers' thirst to still.

Ah cornflowers blue and poppies red,
Weep, for our little Love is dead.

' Hither, come hither, thou fair child,'
Loud sang the water voices wild,
'Come hither, thou delightful boy,
   And tread our cool translucent floors,
Where never scorching heats may come,
   Nor ever wintry tempest roars ;
Nor the sharp tooth of envious age
   May fret thy beauty with decay,

And thou grow sad mid wailful men ;
　But in thy deathless spring-time stay,
Made one with our eternal joy,
For ever an immortal boy.'

Ah cornflowers blue and poppies red,
Weep, for our little Love is dead.

He dipped his pitcher o'er the brink,
About it dimpling sunlights wink,
The smooth rill fills its darkling throat
　With hollow tinklings mounting shrill
And shriller to its thirsty lip ;
　But sweeter, wilder, louder still
The water voices ringing sing ;
　And beckon him, and draw him down
The cool-armed silver-wristed nymphs,
　His warm lips with cold kisses crown ;
And to their chilly bosoms prest,
He sinks away in endless rest.

Ah cornflowers blue and poppies red,
Weep, for our little Love is dead.

But still in the warm twilight eves,

Threading the lone moon-silvered sheaves,

Or where in fragrant dusky heaps

   The dim-seen hay cool scents emits,

The boy across the darkening hills

   Bearing his little pitcher flits,

With feet that light as snowflakes fall,

   Nor, passing, stir the feathered grass ;

And sings a song no man may know,

   Of old forgotten things that pass,

And Love that endeth in a sigh,

And beauty only born to die.

Blue cornflowers weep, red poppies sigh,

For all we love must ever die.

THE SONG.

Birth too and death, slumber and wakefulness, motion and immobility, crowned majesty and squalid filth, discordant clamour and the voice of gods.—EMPEDOCLES.

I.

AN atom of air still hither and thither swung,
Hither and thither tossed and aimlessly flung,
Never at rest on the breath of a passionate song,
A passionate song of love and triumph o'er wrong,
Poured from the trembling lips of the singer afire,
Leaping like flame from the golden heart of the lyre,
A passionate song of triumph !

II.

And ever it mused :
By what law of my being perplexed and confused
Am I tossed thus idly about, nor suffered to rest,
Now in the gulf of the billow and now on its crest,

Hither and thither moved by a Hand in the dark,

Ever to random shocks a wandering mark,

Ever impelled by forces that lie without

In a dance of death that ends in confusion and doubt,

A rhythm of loss, an upward life in defeat,

The onward turned back on its self with death for its
      beat.

III.

And it searched out the laws of vibration, the bound
      and th' impact

Now swift and now slow; and patiently traced out
      each fact

Of its being, how atom with atom ever must meet,

And the limits which still each upward movement
      defeat—

Impassable law that limits the freedom of each.

And still as far as the utmost science could reach

Impulse it found in the lock of mechanical law,

Nought in it all but a backward and forward saw,

Opposite motions that ever each other defeat,

Barren of progress or plan, left still incomplete.

IV.

But the song, the passionate song of triumph and love,

That yet all the while like a living shuttle it wove,

The passionate song of love and triumph o'er wrong,

That conditioned the laws of its wonderful life all
      along,

It knew not nor heard.   For it was but a finite part ;

And the song is the infinite whole, the throb of a
      Heart.

THE SEA-KING.

A ROCK IN SARK.

WHO wrought thee to this semblance of a king,
  Wresting from Thor his hammer and his tool,
Making Olympian lightnings, fashioning
  Thy granite heart with awful thunder shocks
To this majestic shape of kingly rule?
  Who placed thee on thy throne of shattered rocks,
With fateful hands of empire laid asleep
  Upon thy mighty knees, thy stony gaze,
  Thwart which the centuries drift past like haze,
For ever set across a moaning sea?

The sea-birds flap thee with their storm-wet wing,
  Thy calm confusing with tempestuous cries;
The thunder cloud, in darkness gathering,
  Breaks on thy granite neck her groaning heart,

And pours in torrents from thy hollow eyes ;
  The stinging foam swirls ever up athwart
Thy steadfast gaze, and blinds thee with its brine ;
  Grey winter rains across an empty sea
  Lash thee with storm ; but still immutably
Thou ever keep'st that sleepless watch of thine.

What dost thou look for o'er the sea's moist ways,
  What seest thou at eve, or morning prime ?
The birth of slow large stars that stand agaze
  With thee, as one who tells an ancient tale
With one who listening dies to new-born time ?
  The moon's first level splendours trembling pale,
That brim the low sea-caves, slow silvering
  Their wash of darkling waters ?   Or of old
  The sun, who spreads for thee a path of gold,
And bids thee rise and come away, O King ?

Nay, none of these !   Thy far-off gaze doth fall
  Across them, as of one who stares, nor sees,
Waiting a presence from beyond them all ;
  A Light of which they but faint shadows give,

A splendour born of Love, completing these,
  The morn's new birth, fulfilment of the eve.
Thyself a king, thou lookest for a king,
  To reconcile the dawn, still falsified
  By wrong's rude night—beneath his sceptre wide
Love, light, and life made one in endless spring.

Above thy head the great stars wax and wane,
  Beneath thy feet, a deep that ever moans,
The wasteful effort of the wave, the vain
  Slow toil that never overtakes its end ;
About thy ears, the immemorial tones
  Of sea-sung litanies, and chaunts that blend
In some forgotten tongue their solemn psalm,
  And mournful rise to unresponsive skies ;
  A Patience of the rock that never dies,
Through all thine expectation waits in calm.

O Hope that holds the centuries in fee,
  Linking near ill to far-off good for men,
And slighting regent wrong ; dumb prophecy
  That grasp'st the open purpose of the world,

Still writ too large for narrow human ken
    In characters from age to age unfurled ;
Tranced in some ecstasy of thought, I scan
    Thy thunder-stricken features, till they fade
    Invisible to sense, and in thy stead
I gaze upon the marrèd face of Man.

Like thee he looketh for a King to reign ;
    No centuries beguile him of his hope,
Nor congregated wrongs can make it vain,
    That ever break to rise again, and mock
The power that strives with sovereign ill to cope.
    His shattered hope re-forms from every shock,
Weakness invincible of the divine,
    Weak as a wave, yet stronger than the stone,
    As still across his life's confusèd moan,
He waiteth for a King to rise and shine.

Lo, Superstition, Science, Art, each cries,
    ' Me thine allegiance give, the rightful sway,'
Perplexed he clasps their knees, yet from his eyes
    The longing dies not out, the inner dole ;

Discrowned they stand at last, no word have they
   To charm the deep disorder of his soul.
Not till His coming steps in earthquake beat
   The trembling earth, man's rightful Majesty,
   Not until then, O King, will thou and he
Arise, and leap in thunder to His feet.

TWO VOICES.

ABOVE my head, a tideless deep of blue,
Beneath my feet a deep that ever grew.

Two voices on my dreaming ear were borne,
One full of ecstasy, and one forlorn.

The one, the storm-tost sea-mew's plaining cry,
And mocking laugh at all beneath the sky.

Cry of the broken wave, the high endeavour,
That, climbing to its height, sinks baffled ever.

Voice of the weird sea-paths, that winding run
Across the lonely deep, out to the sun ;

Then suddenly break off and disappear,
Nor reach the light, nor lead they anywhere.

Dirge of the bitter springs that bubbling burst,
Tempting the parchèd lips, to slay with thirst.

Wail of sad Love, that to her sun-white breast
Clasps the cold rock that flings her back unblest.

Voice of the Sea whose murmur never wanes,
Heard in the fruited bough, in vernal rains ;

Persistent undertone of life, faint breaths,
That breathe adieu ! adieu ! and still are death's.

Wail of the shipwrecked life, the sea-deep torn,
Of lifted hands, and hearts that sink forlorn.

The other, linking with its glittering chains
Those broken cries, the sky-lark's jubilant strains.

Voice of the cornfields where the children roam,
Whose many winding pathways all lead home.

Shout of the gold of God in harvests given,
The living bread that cometh down from heaven.

Song of the clover-fields, close sweets that lie
Safe stored from all but honeyed heart and eye.

Hymn of the morn that cometh after night,
The dark's negation still affirming light.

Hymn of the eve, still dews, the starry deep,
The Voice that breathes, ' It is enough ; now sleep.'

Song of our Dead, that high in glory walk,
Heard in the pauses of our loved home talk.

Voice of the light, and heaven's own ecstasies,
The loosened passion of the silent skies.

O voices twain, I find you both for ever,
In this deep heart of mine that resteth never.

A deep of pain it is, a deep of light,
I know not whether most 'tis sad or bright.

For but to say that I am glad again,
Is still to find me face to face with pain.

And but to plead no end to life's dull ache,
Is for the bright eternal morn to break.

My sweetest uses spring from saddest tears,
My cloud-born glory sun and tempest wears.

And still my sphere is rolled from dark to light,
Now spins in day, now thunders through the night.

And still two voices to my heart are given,
One of the moaning deep, and one of heaven.

Sark : 1875.

A WAVE.

O BEING in thy dissolution known
    Most lovely then ;
O Life that ever has to die alone,
    To live again ;
O bounding Heart that still must bow and break
    To touch thine end ;
O broken Purpose that must failure take,
    And deathward bend,
For the great tide to stretch from rock to rock
    His shining way ;
O wandering Will that from the furthest shock
    Of sea-deeps grey,
Silver constraint of secret light on high
    Leads safe to shore ;
O living Rapture that dost inly sigh,
    And evermore

Within thy joy the wailful voices keep ;
    I see thee now,
O Son of the unfathomable deep !
    And trembling know
The crownèd Shadow of man's opposites,
    The forces dread
That sway him into being, blanched with lights
    Of thunder bred ;
A poisèd Passion wrought from central breath
    Of whirling storms,
And evermore a deathless life in death,
    That still re-forms.

And thou, man's prototype in varying moods,
    Didst lonely beat
The vacant shores and speechless solitudes
    With silver feet,
Through the great æons wandering forlorn
    In search of him,
As rose and fell like vacant flames, lone morn
    And evening dim,

Ere light had grown articulate in love,
  Or silence knew
Herself as worship. Then didst thou ever move
  Beneath the blue,
An incommunicable mystery,
  About thy shore ;
A visible yearning of the earth and sea,
  That evermore
Flung out white arms to catch at some far good
  Yet unfulfilled,
And failing sobbed and sank in solitude
  With heart unstilled ;
A voice that ever crying as of old
  In deserts dumb,
With hollow tongue reverberate foretold
  A Life to come.

LEAVES.

Leaflet ! leaflet !
Curving to thy lovely limits
   In a cool and peaceful dream,
Like a silver-fringèd ripple,
   Greening to the wet sea-beam ;
By some hidden law conditioned
   Into individual grace,
In green brotherhoods of beauty
Binding all your lovely race.
   Leaflet ! leaflet !
With your gracious tender mouldings,
   Dimpled like an infant's palm,
Ever spread in sweet beseechings
   For the sun and cool dew's balm,
And the charity heaven-breathing
   Of the falling summer rain;

Cool as mothers' healing kisses
　　Falling on our fevered pain ;
Sweeping o'er our hands and foreheads
　　In some quiet woodland place,
　　Tender as the last sad touches
Of our dying on our face.
　　　　Leaflet ! leaflet !
Such a tender thing to look at,
　　Yet with some strange power in thee
To unlock the world's great forces
　　With the sunbeam's golden key,
Power that, loosened from thy child-clasp,
　　Th' avalanche would toss with ease
Back to his high Alpine cradle,
　　Where the printless snowdrifts freeze.
　　　　Leaflet ! leaflet !
With your cool palms shaping ever
　　Out of the invisible,
Out of sun-illumined azure,
　　Hearts of oak that giant swell,
And the great pine's porphyry pillar
　　Reddening with the last red ray ;

In your green and golden leisure,
   Babbling like a child at play.
     Leaflet ! leaflet !
Dear divinest gracious weakness,
   Strong through the invisible,
Strong through laying hold of forces
   That unseen about you dwell ;
Mighty builders of God's temple,
   Who is Light and Who is Power,
Your green guilds for ever rearing,
   Through the drowsy summer hour,
Lovely aisle and branching archway,
   And cool crypts of morning dew,
With the high clere-story windows
   Of the noontide's burning blue ;
Rising into silent worship,
   Like the temple built of old,
Without sound of axe or hammer,
   Rising like a cloud of gold
Into shapes of awful beauty,
   Breathless with the breath of God ;

Ever building through the ages
 Earth her ancient round has trod,
Laying down your lives by myriads,
 So your work may live and grow,
Bearing each your part unknowing
 In the whole too vast to know ;
Then in golden consummation
 Falling like a falling star,
While the autumn winds their requiem,
 Breathe above you from afar.
  Leaflet ! leaflet !
We like you are builders ever
 Of an unseen temple vast,
Building in each high endeavour,
 Building in the silent past,
Now a shrine and now a gargoyle,
 Living stone on stone laid still,
All without a sound arising
 To the master-builder's will :
Every marble pillar built up
 Of a million million lives,

And the sweep of age-long arches,
  As it ever upward strives ;
Till the little part is finished,
  That to the vast whole we lend ;
Then with you we fall together,
  And together touch our end,
    Leaflet ! leaflet !

THE NIGHT AFTER DEATH.

Heart of my heart !
How shall I greet thee ere I sleep this night,
  In that strange far-off land where thou art gone ?
My lips, that faltered not in dark or light
  For tender balms with which to soothe thy spirit's
      moan,
Falter for some high speech and infinite,
  In which to utter sweetness where thou art,
      Dear Heart.

Bid thee good-night ?
As, when the lamps put out, we stood alone
  In the enchanted dusk one moment yet,
And kissed, with hands that locked our lives in one,
  ' Good-night,' then on the wish one last kiss set.

Ah, Love ! there is no night where thou art gone,
　That I should wish thee in thy perfect light,
　　' Good-night.'

　　Bid thee ' farewell,'
Farewell, my Love, farewell for ever now ?
　To thee to whom our utmost well were ill ;
Who farest now where living waters flow,
　With One whose words flow o'er thy spirit still,
And wash life's fever from thee, and the woe
　For which our love could never find the spell,
　　' Farewell.'

　　Or shall I sigh,
Sleep sweet, dear Heart, sleep sweet for evermore ?
　Who needest not to pay away to Death
One half thy day to keep him from thy door ;
　But, gazing into the unknown Beneath,
And bathing in the deep Beyond, dost soar,
　And sing and shine in endless ecstasy
　　On high.

E

Or shall I greet
Thee thus : 'God bless thee as thou blessedst me ? '
Thou whose great light of blessing even now
Has struck me blind, so that I cannot see
Thy face, nor find thy hand, nor touch, nor know,
And darkened all my days with loss of thee.
My blessing would but touch and dim thy feet,
My Sweet.

O Love, my Love !
A beggar girl, I stand alone, ah me !
Alone upon thy palace steps, with all
My faded violets, that once to thee
Were sweet, but sickening now at evenfall,
Smell but of all my want and misery,
While empty hands I stretch to thee, my Love,
My Love !

THE CONTRAST.

ὦ φίλος,
ἆ τὸν ἀεὶ κατὰ γᾶς σκότον εἱμένος.—Sophocles.

LOVE! Love! Love!
The Spring is calling to the earth
In odorous sighings, and the birth
   Of quick warm tears, and kisses heard
When April clouds have wept their fill,
And all the budding woods are still.
   Lo, every secret grove is stirred,
As, o'er the cornfield's tender green,
Her twinkling feet are hurrying seen ;
And Love ! Love ! Love ! she calleth ever
By copse and croft and frozen river.

   Love ! Love ! Love !
The earth is thrilling to the voice
That bids all things rejoice ! rejoice !
   The blind dust yearning to the light,

Bursts into myriad flowery eyes
By beechen roots and grassy rise,
  With silent adoration bright ;
And kindling at the Master's name,
The copse is fledged with delicate flame,
A windblown splendour of the sod,
Burning, yet not consumed, with God.

  Love ! Love ! Love !
The brown grub hiding underground
Hears in his dark the potent sound,
  And quickens at his dreaming heart ;
Twin glories spread on either side,
With the forgotten sunshine dyed.
  And now no more he dwells apart,
No more can darkness tread him down,
A life beyond the grave now grown,
A wandering thought of love become,
He soars—the light his vast sweet home.

  Love ! Love ! Love !
The bird is piping in the brake,
' Awake, dear hearts, awake, awake !

For life is pleasant on the bough.'
While bright eyes watch him from the nest,
A brooding wonder at her breast.
But life must answer love, and now
The pearly caskets open spring,
And soft let out the secret thing,
And all their hidden fairy gold
Is turned to golden songs untold.

Love ! Love ! Love !
My heart is calling with the rest ;
Ah, more than bird or grub unblest !
Ah, less than stick or trodden clay !
My Dead stirs not for any sound,
No glory lifts me from the ground ;
No life, no voice that made my May,
Comes back to my forsaken breast ;
No leaves my kingly sceptre crest ;
My deathless love, howe'er I crave,
Wins but one answer back—a grave.

DRIFT-WOOD.

O SEA-BLEACH'D log that in thy storm-drench'd sleep
    Liest all dark in morning shine,
Forgotten plaything of an alien deep,
    That knows not thee, nor thine.

The ripple's long grey fold in splendour breaks ;
    Far off the sea-gleam's silver line
Shines mystic bright; but thee no light awakes
    From that dark sleep of thine.

Yet once thy long-lost boughs did live and sing.
    And from thy passionate heart, sun fed,
A thousand verdant fancies burst in spring,
    And garlanded thy head.

Fresh dews were thine, the morning's glittering glee ;
    With thee the shy birds housed unseen,

And sang of their delicious loves to thee,
  Wrapped in thy secret green.

But now, flung by wild storms upon the shore,
  No thought of greenness thou dost keep,
But a sea strangeness crusts thee o'er and o'er,
  Weird fancies of the deep.

Dost thou remember, O remember aught
  Of sunny days that once were thine?
And dumbly crave the light, the warmth, in thought,
  Like this sad heart of mine?

Seems the mild murmur of the twilight sea
  The soughing of the evening breeze,
That rocked thy nestlings, and awoke in thee
  Old sea-like melodies?

And rustle round thee, then, thy leafy eaves,
  As when they bloomed in summer bowers,
And purpling thro' thy rain-illumined leaves,
  Gathered the summer showers?

And dost thou, as the vision fades, then know
    The desolation of the light,
The piercing sense of all that is of woe
    By all that was of bright?

Like thee my bough is bare, it wears no green,
    Me storms have overthrown, O tree!
The touch of shipwrecked hands on me hath been,
    Who failed them too like thee.

And yet, tho' not for thee the olden bloom
    Haply upon some human hearth
Thou'lt brightly glow, and lend the winter gloom
    A quiet household mirth.

And haply too the storm-wrecked life may bring
    To some dark hearts a summer glow;
And wake in some sad home a light of spring,
    It never more may know.

May 1868.

VALE! VALE!

LET me go hence !
No leaf but babbles of my hidden grief,
  And makes it common.   Every hedgeway thorn
  Is sharp with it.   The very buds unborn
As soon as opened have it in their eyes ;
And my own footprints, seeking vain relief,
  Meet me in sandy lane, by chalky rise,
  And round again on what their anguish flies—
      Let me go hence !

    Let me go hence,
O woods and fields, all haunted with my Dead !
  Your woodbines beckon up a thought of him ;
  Your dusky gorse's crusted gold is dim
With love departed and with farewell breath ;
Your sparkling seas and lovely valleys spread
  Empty with loss in vacant light beneath
  My feet, and all your sweetness aches with death—
      Let me go hence !

Let me go hence,
Away, away, nor any further wrong
The soul of your fair harmless solitude,
Quickening it with the waste of my own mood,
Till into human pain it sickens fast ;
Nor wake at dead of night to hear along
Your ghostly cliffs, in pauses of the blast,
The sobbings of the unreturning past—
Let me go hence !

Let me go hence !
And down your deep moon-haunted lanes again,
In the warm dusk with glimmering whitethorn sweet,
Lovers will pass with happy lingering feet,
And trail the evening star, by Love held dear,
Thro' your dark leaves ; or from one kiss refrain,
Feeling some tender trouble in the air,
To cry 'Tread soft, some heart has suffered here.'
Let me go hence !

LOVE AND SLEEP AND DEATH.

THOU com'st to me in dreams again
    In that still land our days enfold ;
Lit by our old dead suns, and where
    Our fading wests still keep their gold.

Strange under-world that rounds our sphere,
    And into which our lights go down ;
And all our sunken splendours set,
    To rise again yet fairer grown.

Land of the heart that knows no graves,
    Shaped by the soul that knows not death ;
Where but to love is still to be,
    And drink again life's sweetest breath.

Ah, Love, thou com'st to me unchanged !
 The hand is warm I clasp in mine ;
I kiss no death dews on thy lip,
 No grave-chill wrongs that touch of thine.

No look, no hint of other worlds,
 Confuses me in thy kind eyes ;
Only the old familiar love
 That made my sun at midnight rise.

The awful Shadow that still seems
 To blot us out beneath God's skies,
Light as the shadow of a bird
 From our large life runs off and dies.

Again we walked the woods and fields,
 And paused beside the pleasant farms ;
And trod the sweet, gay-scented paths,
 Alone, with happy love-linked arms.

Again the chestnut spread her palms
 Of benediction o'er our head ;

And birds for love dipped their sweet songs
  Within our sweeter hearts, love fed.

And in the mystic heart of woods
  We sat again, as once, and heard
The ghostly footsteps pattering by,
  And strange leaf-mutterings stirred ;

And sudden sobbings of the breeze,
  That with a passion shook the wood ;
Then died in infinite farewells
  Upon the murmurous solitude.

And there I sang to thee the songs,
  Where thine and mine no death can part ;
And into thy glad breast shook out
  The sweetness of my woman's heart.

The same, and yet, ah, not the same !
  Something was changed, I knew not whence :
Our love had gained some growth of tears,
  A sad, divine significance ;

An aching tenderness that sobbed
    Against the doors of speech, and lo,
From all the windows of my soul
    Looked forth with angel eyes aglow.

Something I did not understand,
    I breathed but a diviner air ;
Some veil of life was rent, and all
    Love's dear divinity lay bare.

I could not look at thy dear face,
    But straight God's dew baptised it there ;
I could not utter thy loved name,
    But still it seemed an answered prayer.

Our commonest act—the food we shared—
    Grew sacramental to my soul ;
Thy lightest touch, thine idlest word,
    Long lonely years of pain made whole.

Love, by some pain as deep as He,
    Some lone, dread, agonistic strife,

Now knew himself as Love indeed,
  And Death but as an added life.

And in that strange new glory set,
  My lightest fault I could not bear ;
But, falling on thy neck, I cried :
  'Forgive that e'er I grieved thee, Dear.'

Then didst thou bow thy lips on mine,
  And, in that rapture of held breath,
I woke, and knew by its great light
  My love had seen the face of Death.

ON A WHITE BUTTERFLY.

Thou exquisite frail thing of life and light,
That tak'st with sudden ecstasy my sight !
   Art thou some flower enamoured of a star,
That in some pause of woodland leaves each night
   Shone mildly on her from afar?

And loving so, and yearning so all day,
And having prayed, one early dawn in May,
   Her simple soul grew loose to earth that bore
Her whiteness, heavenward floating soft away,
   And her green place knew her no more.

Thou exquisite white flower-soul ! what place may be
'Mid the rude forces of our world for thee,
   That split the frozen crag with winter wan,
And pour the sounding cataracts of the sea,
   And shatter the deep heart of man ?

Nay, the great world grows tender for thy sake,
All things for thee a finer issue take ;
   The blast that rends the pine and sways the deep,
Tames his rude hand to rock thy leaf, nor break
   The cradle of thy honeyed sleep.

The storm whose breath along the hillside smokes,
And all the sunburnt valleys drenching soaks,
   Spares the light dust upon thy wing ; and fleet
Dread thunderbolts, that blanch the heart of oaks,
   Drop harmless at thy feeble feet.

Fearless thou launchest forth when loud winds roar,
Safe when our mighty ships are seen no more,
   Sailing the treacherous ocean of the air ;
Thy light skiff shoots from flowery shore to shore :
   For thee the winds are always fair.

Each flower to thee glad recognition flings,
Kissing the freckled inward of thy wings ;
   The rose for thee a bridal bed of old
Makes of her bosom's crimson curtainings,
   Thy dower all her secret gold.

Thou fallen blossom from the Tree of Life,
Drifted into a world with gravestones rife
  By some chance air across the Guarded Gate,
With our mortality at joyous strife,
  With thine own paradise elate.

Was it a wonder holy men of old,
As yet our streets were paved with heavenly gold,
  With pious care inscribing ancient lore,
Lit with thy poisèd loveliness untold
  Some stern old prophet-truth of yore ?

Faint with the centuries, man's ancient trust
And hope divine seem written in the dust ;
  New science bids him hug a phantom show,
Nor the divinity within him trust,
  Nor aught of deathless being know.

But fresh as in the primal morn thou art,
With the immortal in us taking part ;
  Thy wing's light flicker flouts at Death o'erbold,
Uttering the glad resurgam of our heart,
  The dear white joyous faiths of old.

Methinks that God has set His weakest thing,

In loving scorn, refutal glad to fling

   At all our human wisdom that denies ;

And with our dear Hope weighted thy frail wing

   For that loved dust that silent lies.

Token thou art of God's great tenderness,

Fresh courage giving me to live and bless,

   Trusting my dear ones unto Him to save,

Who tempers all things to thy feebleness,

   Nor left thee in the silent grave.

Goodbye, sweetheart ! light-winged thou dost depart,

Divinest lessons leaving in my heart,

   Love, victor over Doubt and Death at length.

For one of the weak things of God thou art,

   Stronger than man in all his strength.

GREEN GRAVES.

Not the summer rain that falleth,
　Slipping from its purple sheath,
With the freshness of the meadows
　Borne upon its heaven-sweet breath ;
Not the warm drops green leaves gather,
　Dipping their cool dimpled palms
In the runnels of the shower,
　Till some rush of loosened balms
From the windward field-beds blowing,
　Shakes the sun-struck jewels down,
Pattering on the churchyard dock leaves,
　With pink mallow overblown ;
Not the dews at shut of daylight
　When from the grey dreaming tower,
Darkly keen against the evening,
　Tolls the dim leaf-muffled hour ;

Not the moon's cool dropping silver,

   Rippling through light aspen shade ;

Not the dawn's unfooted freshness,

   Pearling every tender blade ;

Nay, not one of these, I ween,

   Keeps our graves so fresh and green.

But a secret shower falling,

   Ever falling night and day ;

Tender names we never uttered,

   Hustled in life's press away ;

Precious words of fond affection,

   All too late, and breathed in vain,

Dear regrets for love unspoken,

   Wild regrets for spoken pain ;

Tears that wash the blindness from us,

   Holden eyes that knew them not,

Till great Death revealed our angels,

   Life defaced, confused, forgot ;

Passionate kisses never given,

   Frozen buds all choked with snow,

Dying with their locked-up sweetness,
　　Love's completeness ne'er to know ;—
Such a precious heaven-sweet shower,
　　As had made a lifetime green,
Made the dead hearts burst in blossom,
　　Unto them dear heaven had been ;
　　　Now cold rain with nought to save,
　　　Greening but a senseless grave.

THE WORLD OF MIGHT-HAVE-BEENS.

OFTTIMES I fondly dream could there but be
    A world betwixt this world and that Unknown,
With its vast reaches of eternity,
    Its unimagined light, and splendours lone.

A world where broken things of Earth's delight
    Might bloom again, and every ' might-have-been '
Might be ; as chilly rains of yesternight
    But as the morning's pride of dew are seen.

A little world in the great starry sweep
    Scarce seen, that rises in a rosy west,
And trembles on the children's early sleep,
    On silver tiptoe not to break their rest.

God's casket for lost kisses, farewell breath,
    Sad sighs that only shook a withered leaf,

The dim sweet touches of thin hands in death,
　　Heart-hungers that on earth found no relief.

A little world all grassy cool, and green,
　　Where feet that this world's burning marls have trod,
Or blistered with its dewless highways been,
　　Might cool themselves against the daisied sod.

Where darling buds, their lips all black with frost,
　　Might balmy drink once more the warm spring rain,
And broken eggs moss-strewn, their spring-songs lost,
　　Might round into the sea-green pearl again.

And lovely souls walled up in graceless clay,
　　That still contemns the angel-guest within,
Sweet souls that never here have had their day,
　　Nor lover's kiss, nor clinging child might win ;

Yet grew not sour, nor struck at hungry fate,
　　But patient in their stony niche upcurled,
Of the great human Sorrow made their mate,
　　And dropped their bruisèd spikenards on the world.

Might they find there the joys they knew not here,
  Like friends we missed, who by some shorter way
Got safe home first, not lost, but waiting there,
  To greet our wayworn feet with welcomes gay.

And there to meet our Dead beneath old skies,
  Not changed, but just the same ; no angel bright
To vex with unfamiliar light the eyes
  Grown dim with weeping for them thro' the night ;

But ah, the same ; th' old hands we clasped in ours,
  Whose touch could ease life's ache and fretful strain ;
The comfortable voice that in dark hours
  Rang out the evensong of all our pain.

Not lost in light, but set about once more
  With all the homely sweetness of our earth ;
The old familiar fields, the sounding shore,
  Dear night and morning kisses, household mirth.

Only upon our lips the supreme kiss
  Would blossom still to guard from loveless breath

The gate of life, and in our midmost bliss
   Last looks in eyes would deepen love with death.

Till every silver issue of the morn
   Broken on earth had clasped a golden end,
And kissed a perfect rose had every thorn,
   And every friend had utmost loved with friend ;

Then like a star that lingers, glinting through,
   'Mid sweet hedge-rose and evening-lighted grass ;
But rising beats at length the wider blue—
   To kiss, and unto other worlds to pass.

TO THE GOLDEN ALPINE
HEARTSEASE.

DEAR HEART, I found among our English dews
   When piped the bitter north wind shrill,
Clad like a mourner in thy purpling hues,
   Standing all dark and chill ;

All dark but for that tender hint of dawn
   About that glooming heart of thine,
A secret spring within thy breast withdrawn,
   Ever half quenched to shine ;

Have thy sad thoughts gone golden in the light,
   That secret spring of dawn let out
To flood thy life, since thou didst climb this height
   Above our pain and doubt ?

Since thou hast on the eternal whiteness gazed,
    That changeless takes no print of man,
Love's pillar high of rosy fire upraised
    Since morn and eve began ;

Here on this Alpine pasture flowery fair,
    Sparkling and fresh with mountain rains,
Where the cool silence of the thin sweet air
    Unbroken still remains ;

Save for the kine-bells tinkling on the hill,
    Or grasshoppers clad in viewless green,
Clashing their little silver cymbals shrill
    In ceaseless praise unseen.

Thou and my Love all shining in the light,
    My Love who climbed the heights with thee,
Far, far above all hills, beyond the night,
    Beyond our vexèd sea ;

And left me but a darkened memory
    With which to face the orphaned hours,
Alone in all this sick perplexity,
    We call this life of ours.

The Shadow of thine unseen loveliness,

Fresh with the dews of thine eternal youth,

As with bowed head I worship and adore

Love's radiant Heart in seven-hued light laid bare.

Bow of the depths, not of the sun-crowned heights !

Set with my loved lost jewels cruel Death

Wrung from my trembling grasp and writhen hands ;

The glory of my Dead I seek in vain

In constellated sun and sleepless star,

Treading with devious foot my darkened days ;

My hidden bow that in the secret place

Of thunder shines, kept in high heaven for me.

Bow of the deep dark underworld of woe,

That underlies life's shining surfaces,

Dim populous pain and multitudinous toil,

Unheeded of the heedless world that treads

Its piteous upturned faces underfoot,

In the gay rout that rushes to its ends.

Ah radiant unseen heart of darkest things,

That is not dark, nor waste expense of tears,

Nor void, but sevenfold glory of the light ;

Promise for all the broken-hearted here,

The sad, the poor, the sinful, and despairing,

Dark lives whose sorrow, like a caverned wave,

Falters and sobs about its pent-in walls,

Nor ever breaks a glory in the sun.

Ah hidden splendour, I behold thee not !

Where stands thy jewelled arch triumphant, lo,

I see but leaden wrack, and beating storm,

And the fierce light that has the keys of death.

But once in time in this calm sea of glass,

That Love has spread before his mountain throne,

I have beheld, let down from heaven to earth,

Thy secret light, and know henceforth for ever

In darkest things the hidden Bow is there.

THE SYMPATHY OF NATURE.

'The earnest expectation of the creature waiteth for the manifestation of the sons of God.'

SWEET Bird, that mid the sunlights of the leaf
  Singest where hazel-tufts thy shape conceal,
Who told thee of this secret pain, this grief
    That long ago both tears and words outwore,
    Love, dead with waiting at a closèd door,
      Dumb arms outstretched in infinite appeal ?
        Ah simple soul, I told it not to thee,
  Yet thou hast guessed it all among the leaves,
Uttering it all in some sad speech divine,
Till from my heart it flows away to thine,
And thence to all the lonely dells is given
In plaintful tones whose sweetness dies in heaven,
    While thy melodious heart leaf-hidden grieves,
      Breaking for me, dear Heart, for me !

G

2

Fair Flower, that in that greening nest of thine,
 Through harmless days dost draw thy harmless
   breath,
What dost thou know of this sad heart of mine,
 This alien birth of sad humanity,
 Whose early glories were but born to die,
 That ever keeps reluctant tryst with Death ?
   Ah simple Heart, I told it not to thee ;
 Thou on th' untarnished silver of thy leaf
Dost lightly wear the heavy centuries
Of wrong, renewing thy young loveliness
With every Spring, not knowing Death ; and yet
With orient tears thy shining lids are wet,
 Through which thou look'st responsive to my grief,
  Weeping for me, dear Heart, for me !

3

O Cuckoo, jocund brother of the Spring,
 What knowest thou, ah thou, of wintry wrong,
Of leafless boughs where once the heart did sing
 Among the green, all faded now and gone,

Of kindly looks chill Death has turned to stone,

Of empty nests left desolate of song?

  Ah vagrant Voice, I told it not to thee :

Yet like a distant bell thy constant note

Tolls for the ancient Springs that are no more,

' Farewell ! farewell ! ' it tolleth o'er and o'er,

' Farewell,' from lifted lawn and secret dell,

 We live in light, we love thee still, farewell ; '—

 Voice of my Loved upon the air afloat

  Thou art to me, dear Heart, to me !

4

O Wind, that heavy with Spring fragrance dies,

 Slow sweetening all the glades and dingles nigh,

What dost thou know of bitter human sighs,

 Longings that never taste the fruited tree,

 And Hope a butterfly blown out to sea,

 Fainting with flight, yet settling but to die ?—

  Ah spirit sweet, I told it not to thee,

 Yet hark ! mysterious murmurs blend with thine,

Infinite whispers of some far-off good

Stir the deep heart of the green solitude,

And every leaf is seized with prophecy,
And somewhere flights of angels sweep me by,
　　As thou dost die upon the hush divine,
　　　　Sighing for me, dear Heart, for me !

5

And O ye hills, grey woods, and far-off vale,
　　That dim the gaze with too, too happy light,
Where all life's fevered fret and toil and wail,
　　And all the fading cries of fading men,
　　Are drowned in azure peace beyond our ken,
　　That laps your windless woods and homesteads
　　　　white ;
　　　　Fair Loveliness, I told it not to thee,
　　Yet to my brooding sense and fancy fond
A patient sadness holds the valleys dumb,
A silent waiting as for things to come,
Some open secret bringing in the day,
And all your footless pathways lead away
　　To some deep hidden bliss, a Rest beyond,
　　　　A Home for me, dear Hearts, for me !

THE WAYSIDE ANGEL.

DEATH, we once pictured thee a sheeted horror,
    A bloodless thing compact of bones and dust,
    On all life's fairest gold a cankering rust,
But by our Easter suns we see thee truer ;
    Thou a familiar presence now art grown
    And as Love's white-winged messenger art known.

Sometimes thy feet are set among the lilies,
    And in the dawn we see thee passing by,
    In thy deep bosom lulling tenderly
A sleeping child, while life falls off and sorrow,
    As from the pendant slackening finger-tips
    The bluebell or the fading primrose slips.

Or through the ripening corn at noon thou goest,
    Leading with pious care some aged feet
    Back to fresh youth, and home, and springtime sweet.

The reaper as thou passest stays his reaping
  And musing feels thy breath like softest air
  Blow cool upon his brow and lift his hair.

Or in the burning meads of June thou sittest
  Mid the sweet-scented swathes of dying flowers,
  Dying in their fresh prime of morning hours ;
While in thy lap some fairer garden-blossom
  Of human hopes has slumbering laid her head,
  Heavy with precious dews by sad eyes shed.

Or o'er some wayworn form we see thee bending,
  Giving a draught from thy cool pitcher's brink
  From those deep wells that quench, to all who drink,
All mortal thirst and weariness and longing ;
  And straightway the lame feet gain strength to go
  A vaster way where swiftest thought is slow.

Angel beloved of all the broken-hearted !
  Seen through thy veil old burning pains show grey
  As a forgotten lamp surprised by day ;

Life's dull-leaved book gilds as we softly close it :
    And not the dark, we feel, but endless light
    Is Life's great end and issue infinite.

Sorrow runs to thine arms as child to mother,
    And with her hand in thine endures the night ;
    And Love before thee keeps his garments white.
And, hallowing all, thy Presence bendeth o'er us,
    Like that faint hueless evening sky we see,
    That has the promise of the stars to be.

TO ROBERT HERRICK.

'A funeral stone
  Or verse I covet none,
But only crave
  Of you that I may have
A sacred laurel springing from my grave.'

Herrick.

THOU sweet old poet, jocund gay,
  Fresh as an English spring-time seen,
With her moist meadow-gleams, her grey
  Half dipped in golden green ;
And rain-lit lanes bestrewn at warm noon-day
With rosy dimples of the fallen May.

Thou who didst win thy daffodils
  To loose their tongues of flame, and tell
The charm that hid thee from our ills,
  And bade sad thoughts farewell ;

The golden secret of their deathless joy
No leaden-footed winters can destroy.

So thou and joy were boonest friends,
　　Thy days had all a golden rise,
And dying, touched on golden ends ;
　　While thou beneath spring skies
Didst fling thy careless glory down the years,
That come to us so chill and grey with tears.

But now, thy golden eves all done,
　　Thy daffodils and thou for ever
Long since to evensong have run,
　　And gone away together,
Leaving all moist dim places of the earth
An afterglow of all your harmless mirth ;

Hast thou thy wish, O jocund soul,
　　In thy green western resting-place ?
No weight of stone with sculptured scroll
　　To crush thy breezy grace,
And hide thee from thy daisies newly blown,
And into blatant darkness tread thee down.

But that green monument of thine,
    A laurel tree above thy head,
  Scattering her harmless lights divine
    About thy darkened bed ;
Or pattering silver litanies by the hour,
As sweet as thine, beneath the falling shower.

  Or haply standing mute and chill
    At the dark break of day, thy tree
  Feels through her leaves a mystic thrill,
    A wind of prophecy.
'Lie still, dear Heart,' thy Daphne sighs to thee,
I feel the dawn ; thy Christ comes presently.

A GARDEN OF GIRLS.

A RUSH of maidens from a garden porch,
  All clad in virginal and festive white.
And while I stood agaze within the lane
  At all the wonder of them, and delight,
As strong winds pour a rush of morning blue
  Through thick-leaved trees, great joy was in me
      born ;
'The world is young,' I cried, ' and in his prime ;
  'The golden age comes back each golden morn.'

And singing, one whirled round in mazy dance,
  With palpitating feet that lightly beat
The quivering blades as thick as thunder drops,
  When all the purpling hills are faint with heat ;
And through her shadow swift the daisies streamed
  Like flights of meteors through a summer night ;
While silver laughter shook the aspens hoar,
  And all the kingcups nodded with delight.

And one tossed up a history book in sport ;
    Old empires rose and fell at her sweet will
And the rich dust of buried kings and queens
    Upon her light-aired fancy eddied still ;
And lo, the ages' sequent toil and pain
    Were tumbled into ecstasies of May,
And all the garnered sorrow of the world
    Flashed at her touch into a maiden's play.

And two their radiant heads together leant—
    One black as pods of broom, the other seemed
The broom in flower—and babbled, as they strolled,
    Love-secrets from all eyes safe hidden deemed ;
Two babbling brooks close huddled up in flowers,
    That yet unknown had slipped their covert green,
And caught faint snatches of the starry sky,
    Of vast beyonds, and world on world unseen.

But one paused close to where I darkling stood
    Leaf-hidden—fairest she of all the band—
And to the white shell of her ear she made
    A rosy lip with one fair lifted hand,

As rapt she listened to the nightingale,
  That in some ecstasy of love and pain,
Broke his wing'd heart among the beechen leaves,
  And linked our souls together in the lane.

Then as he ceased, on one soft knee she fell,
  To succour some belated, weary thing—
A little downy caterpillar 'twas,
  That piteous took those eyes of early spring,
And from her honeysuckle finger-tips
  Outstretched to her its wavering length forlorn,
And plaintive blind face feeling for the light,
  Till laid at rest beneath the blossoming thorn.

When sudden to her lovely height she rose,
  Spreading her sweet palms sunward to the air,
As though the angel in her, all unknown,
  For all lost souls and sad stood suppliant there,
Breathing a prayer too deep for consciousness ;
  For her girl lips but cried 'It rains ! run ! run !'
And like a flight of white-winged birds they passed,
  And left me standing darkened in the sun.

But now she waits my voice, my coming step ;
For these she listens, sweeter to her ear
Than ever nightingale's enchanted moan ;
And all hurt, helpless things she holdeth dear
And in her balmy bosom stills their pain ;
And none, to drive her from my side, may cry
'It rains,' for in her love without a cloud
I walk, no longer lonely, till I die.

THE CHILDREN'S BEDTIME.

THE clock strikes seven within the hall,
   The curfew of the children's day,
To call each little vagrant foot
   From dance and song and livelong play ;
Their day that in our wider light,
Floats like a silver day-moon white,
Nor in our darkness sinks to rest,
But sets within a golden west.

Ah tender hour ! that sends a drift
   Of children's kisses through the house,
And cuckoo-notes of sweet ' Good-night,'
   That thoughts of heaven and home arouse ;
And a soft stir to sense and heart,
As when the bee and blossom part ;
And little feet that patter slower,
Like the last droppings of the shower.

And in the children's rooms aloft
   What blossom shapes do gaily slip
Their dainty sheaths, and rosy run
   From clasping hand, and kissing lip,
A naked sweetness to the eye,
Blossom and babe and butterfly
In witching one, so dear a sight !
An ecstasy of love and light.

And ah, what lovely witcheries
   Bestrew the floor ! an empty sock,
By vanished dance and song left loose
   As dead birds' throats ; a tiny smock,
That sure upon some meadow grew,
And drank the heaven-sweet rains ; a shoe
Scarce bigger than an acorn cup,
Frocks that seem flow'ry meads cut up.

Then, lily-dressed in angel-white,
   To mother's knee they trooping come
The soft palms fold like kissing shells,
   And they and we go singing home ;

Their bright heads bowed and worshipping,
As though some glory of the spring,
Some daffodil that mocks the day,
Should fold his golden palms and pray.

The gates of paradise swing wide
   A moment's space in soft accord,
And those dread angels, Life and Death,
   A moment vail the flaming sword ;
As o'er the weary world forlorn,
From Eden's secret heart is borne,
That breath of paradise most fair,
By mothers called, 'the children's prayer.'

Ah deep pathetic mystery !
   The world's great woe unconscious hung
A rain-drop on a blossom's lip,
   White innocence that wooes our wrong,
And Love divine that looks again,
Unconscious of the cross and pain,
From sweet child-eyes ; and in that child
High heaven and sad earth reconciled.

H

Then kissed we lay them down on beds
　　As fragrant white as clover sod,
And all the upper floors grow hushed
　　With children's sleep and dews of God.
And as our stars their beams do hide,
The stars of twilight, opening wide,
Take up the heavenly tale at even,
And light us home to God and heaven.

A BACK-STREET CHILD.

FROM LIFE.

A LANE that stints God's boundless charity,
  Of open sky around, afar,
Down to one narrow strip of changeless sky
  That scarce can hold a lingering star.

A house that like a wicked old age leers
  From casements at the passers-by,
Opening on loveless brawls and human speech
  That fouls its own divinity.

The very walls seemed cursed with human sin,
  No Bible pictures smiling fair
Looked down, no Saviour's face of love and grief—
  The rat ran careless riot there.

And drearily I counted o'er and o'er
   The dingy splotches on the wall ;
What touch of God is here to make me feel
   On hallowed ground my footsteps fall ?

Yet even there God had not left Himself
   Without a witness undefiled ;
For in that bare unlovely tenement
   Did there not dwell a little child ?

Amid coarse sights and coarser sounds she grew
   Touched with a beauty of the skies ;
As clean and bright as starry river buds
   From the black bottom-oozes rise.

Hidden, like the great Seer's spirits blest,
   In her own light from ill without,
Her heart, a singing fountain of delight,
   All day her happy thoughts shook out.

Oft wild with glee she beat the dusty flags,
   Heard not the brawling voices chime,

Heard but the angels singing in her heart,
   And with her little feet kept time.

No toys had she, that child, no waxen babes
   To cuddle to her infant breast ;
A child, yet thrilling to a woman's bliss,
   Both babe, and baby-mother blest.

And yet she nothing lacked, nay, for the Lord
   Was shepherd to His lamb ; for her
His living waters gushed in stifling streets,
   And ever springing pastures were.

For to her love all things seemed beautiful,
   And those foul splotches on the wall
A band of rosy scholars oft she made,
   Each blotch on her sweet heart a call.

And with her small pink finger-tip held up
   She'd sit before them smiling gay,
And cry, ' Now, pretty dears, be good, be good,
   And all your little lessons say.'

Ah, light of God that shineth everywhere !
   If ere man all unlovely seems,
A broken thing from which Thy life has run,
   And left but dust and dusty dreams ;

I ask no richer gift than that child's heart,
   To which all in Thy light appears ;
And even the rude splotches on the wall,
   Bathed in its love grow ' pretty dears.'

Blind me with seeing tears, until I see
   In meanest things Thy beauty lies ;
And God's great poetry is everywhere,
   To open hearts and love-lit eyes.

THE HIDDEN ONES.

FAIR souls there are that in dark alleys hide,
In anguish and forsakenness abide,
  Reft of all good, and fed on tears, with pain,
Lord of the house, who yet like stars alway
Do walk the darkness in eternal day.

Their words ring out upon the listening ear,
Like some sweet Angelus we haply hear,
  Borne upwards from dim valleys drenched in storm,
Telling us, as we climb the mountain stair,
That the dear God is keeping watch down there.

For in their hearts blooms Faith, the mystic birth,
That rooted grows from darkest things of earth,
  Like that strange sea-rose nursed on bitter dews,
Unsunned, and beaten by tempestuous swells,
That blossoms in the lonely heart of shells.

τὸ φανερούμενον φῶς.

A METEOR, flaming on its way,
Struck the dark world with sudden day,
While all men slept, then passed away.

A lover woke, and murmuring cried :
' The day ! that brings her to my side,
Brings to mine arms her maiden pride.'

A midnight wrestler paused in prayer :
' 'Tis He ! the day of wrath is here !
Wake ye that sleep, repent and fear !'

A sick girl turned her sleepless eye :
' Are flights of angels passing by,
So great a light is in the sky?'

A rich man started from his bed :
' A fire ! my wealth consumes ! ' he said,
' My garnered fields to heaven flame red.'

A little child its arms outswept,
With upturned face, and ' Mammy ' wept,
Then turned upon its side and slept.

DAISIES.

My dreaming eyes were set in some deep trance
    Of Love and Pain, when in her own great light
The soul is shut in on herself, with glance
    That, seeing, sees not fairest outward sight,
        Ear that unhearing hears ;

When in the mystic house some smooth-hinged door
    Swung wide, and all your innocent white throng
Came crowding in upon the sense, and o'er
    Me swept in vision beautiful and strong,
        And blessed me unawares.

Ye stood white-wingèd each as stars at dawn,
    Like shining hosts of young-eyed cherubim,
In breathless adoration sunward drawn,
    Your faces turning all one way to Him,
        Who makes your endless day.

Each star seemed ready for a heavenward flight,
  But as fond mothers bid their darlings go,
Yet lest they go too far still clasp them tight,
  One little stem still held you fast below,
    Lest ye should soar away ;

Lest ye should own the kinship of your birth,
  And join your starry sisters of the skies,
And leave all desolate our starless earth,
  That never more should see your opening eyes
    Among her orphan dews.

So meek your one green tie to us ye own,
  Keeping your glad epiphanies in the dust,
And from our cradle to our grave unknown,
  Dear new nativities of love and trust
    Into our hearts infuse.

Star of our childhood pure, ere yet we had
  Outgrown the lily, all our thoughts as white
As when your round and happy faces bade
  ' Good morning ' to us, brothers in delight,
    From morn till shut of day.

And with your heavenly treasure rust nor thief
 Corrupts we filled our dimpled hands with glee,
And one dew fell upon our sleep at eve,
 And one rose-flush of slumbering infancy
  Upon our faces lay.

And yours the first light chains of earth we wore,
 Fair flowery chains of our lost paradise,
Who since have known such heavy chains and sore
 Of sin and death and dire necessities,
  Iron whose rust is blood.

Yet those first chains perchance a promise were,
 Forecasting for us a necessity,
That still is perfect freedom, ordered fair—
 Love's golden chain that whoso wears is free,
  Self-motioned unto good.

Up with the day our paths of toil ye grace ;
 Still turning to the light, your honest eye
Bids us be plain and high as Truth's own face,
 And with white deeds and sunbright chastity
  Our golden manhood crown.

And all the footprints of our joy ye set
 In orient pearls, and on our griefs ye shine
A star of hope upon our eyelids wet,
 Just touched with some new rose of dawn divine,
  New life will make our own.

And when old age has bowed us and we look
 Up to the stars no more, but track the dust,
Still ye forsake us not ; by field and brook
 Our childhood's star shines back old love and trust,
  And light our worn feet home.

Nor even then when the last prayer is said,
 And the last lingering footstep dies away,
Do ye forsake the place where Love is laid,
 But o'er his grave keep humble watch each day,
  Till the great dawning come.

Angel or flower shall I call you, sweets ?
 Who share the long lone watchings of the heart,
Trimming your deathless lamps in winter sleets
 And summer suns with the wise virgins' art,
  To keep Love's vigils there.

Till looking back from other worlds of light,
    Our earth may show, like you, a mild white star,
And night and death, and tempest in the night,
    Be seen a wandering spot rose-fringed afar,
        With morn and evening fair.

A FLOOD IN SPRING.

ALL night the roaring dark fell loud
  About the streaming storm-lashed eaves ;
All night the darkened panes were swashed
  With dripping sprays of ivy-leaves.

All night upon the rocking bough
  The bird sat close to the wet nest ;
Nor felt the windy grey drenched dawn
  Thrill into song within her breast.

All night the voiceless meadow brooks,
  The silver secrets of the mead,
Guessed at but by the crowding flowers,
  Rose in their plashy beds of reed.

Till on that glittering morn of May
  We rose up to the strangest sight—
The waters out from vale to vale,
  May-meadows flooded in a night.

Beneath our loved old meadow trees
 The summer sky spread broad and bright ;
The daisies drowned in morning blue,
 All went to heaven in the night.

And every bird that beats the air
 Had now a phantom brother dear,
That flies with him through fairer skies,
 And sings a song no man can hear.

And silver footed clouds slow pace
 The path to church across the fields ;
And everywhere the strong brown earth
 To visionary depths now yields.

And all our old familiar gates
 That let us through but yester morn
To field-paths rambling through the dew,
 And glades all blanched with fragrant thorn :

Now open but to ghostly hands
 On footless depths of rosy dawn,

And moist blue chasms of burning noon,
  And sunset hollows deep withdrawn.

And the great stars come down at night,
  And walk with men upon the earth,
As when the sons of morning sang
  Of all fair things the primal birth.

Old Saturn with his belts of fire
  Majestic treads our pastures fair,
And the sweet sister Pleiades
  Stream through the glen with golden hair.

And where we toiled now floats the cloud,
  And where we wept now burns the star ;
And from our narrow vexed to-day
  Open calm infinites afar.

And all our common beaten paths
  Without a sound now break away,
And show God's heaven of love beneath,
  And in our dust fresh springs of day.

I

ON A DEAD ROBIN IN A CHURCH.

WHAT, dead, dear heart? thy throat, so dainty sweet,
    Limp as Long Purples [1] of the meadow grass,
    Laid low and fading where the mowers pass ;
                 Thy pretty feet
Curled up, their tender trefoils shut beneath
                   Chill dews of death.

Must never more against the wintry west
    Thy thin sweet song be heard beside our door,
    Piping of spring amid the branches hoar ?
                Thy ruffled breast
Red as a russet beech-leaf in the sun,
               When day is done.

[1] ' There with fantastic garlands did she come, of crow-flowers, nettles, daisies, and long purples' (*Hamlet*, Act III., Sc. VII.) The common meadow orchis.

Many rude storms thou knew'st, thou tender thing,
  Many a roaring dark about thy bed,
  No stouter roof above thy harmless head
                 Than thine own wing,
And God's great care for thee His little one,
          Who faileth none.

Yet here within this cool and silent place
  Thou need'st must find thy death where souls find
    life,
  And windless calms amid the tempests strife,
               And heaven's own grace.
Our tenderest balms but bruise thy harmless head,
          And leave thee dead.

How was it, Dear ?   These jewelled panes o'erhead
  Didst take for the rich summer dawns divine,
  That filled those dark leaf lattices of thine
              With trembling red ;
And flying upwards those strange splendours dread
          Did strike thee dead ?

Or seemed these quaint carved figures, lying prone,
　　Thine own dear babes grown old, and dead to
　　　　fame,
　　Grown old waiting a love that never came,
　　　　　　　　And turned to stone?
Freezing thy life-blood in thy balmy breast
　　　　　　　　With their cold rest.

Or didst thou recognise again the Woe,
　　That erst thy pious breast did ruddy stain,
　　And fling thyself against the pictured pane
　　　　　　　　In vain, nor know
But blessed beams now pierce those hands and side
　　　　　　　　With ruby dyed?

Or broke thy heart alone for thy loved haunts,
　　Thy daisies that one touch of crimson makes
　　Akin with thee, thy meads, thy bosky brakes,
　　　　　　　　And woodland chaunts?
All thy wide life of pastures, wood, and rosy sky,
　　　　　　　　Left, here to die.

Couldst thou not stay and let us sing together ?
   Thy world, that like a raindrop on a thorn
   No shadow casts, and our great world forlorn,
               That casteth ever
The shadow, Death, and in heaven's topmost height
             Behold, 'tis night.

Or did the golden throats that throb in thunder
   With man's great adoration and his pain,
   O'erpower thine, shatter thy simple strain,
              And break asunder
Thy glad child-hymns, and daisy-linkèd days,
             With vaster praise ?

I know not ; only that thy life was caught
   Within a vaster life that shut thee in
   With thunders and with lightnings, death and sin ;
              And thou distraught
Didst dash thyself against that alien light,
             And die that night.

IN AMONG THE WHEAT.

In among the wheat, in among the wheat,
She and I wandered one eve in the sun;
Blue-dim in the gold the pathway did run
      Through cornfield and farm;
Splendours streamed up from the earth at our feet,
Wind-shaken flames of amber-stemmed wheat,
   Splendours streamed down from the west golden-
     warm,
Earth and sky met in one deep tender glow;
   With them it was evening, rich and complete,
With us 'twas chill dawn, as we wandered on slow
      In among the wheat.

In among the wheat, in among the wheat,
The path was so narrow that ran through the dew,
No room as we went was there ever for two,
      So I led the way;

Whispers i' the wheat, and whispers i' the heart,

As silently loving we walked on apart ;

   'Loves she me? hates she me? will she say nay?'

'Hush my heart! hush my heart! hush though thou

    break.'

   The corn-daisies winked golden-eyed at our feet,

'Fool that he is, not to trust us and speak,

     In among the wheat.'

   In among the wheat, in among the wheat,

Hearing her, feeling her garments' soft play,

I walked on by heart, not by sight, all the way,

     For with her was my sense ;

Till we reached where a stile makes a flowery bay,

'Twixt two golden tides that soft up to it sway—

   Coming up through the wheat, then I watched

    her from thence,

Slipping her low golden cloud like a star,

   And flushing, all rosy, right up to my feet,

Then waiting my help to climb the stile's bar,

     In among the wheat.

In among the wheat, in among the wheat,
Up in my arms I took her, and laid
The whole of my life on her lips' budded red,
          In one exquisite kiss.
Deep golden laughter took hold of the wheat,
That rippled and rippled, and broke at our feet ;
          The corn-daisies stared, wide-eyed, at our bliss,
And high up by himself in the roseate glow
          The lark wild for joy sang sweet, sweet, sweet,
Of ineffable things going on down below
          In among the wheat.

In among the wheat, in among the wheat ;
Gone was the stile, left behind, and passed by,
But the kiss still remained, as my love and I
          Went soft on our way.
Golden was the west, and golden the corn,
And golden, O golden our love's opening morn,
          Where our two hearts in shining made but one day ;
And though narrow the path that ran through the dew,
          So close now we walked, so close and so sweet,
That somehow we found room enough for us two
          In among the wheat.

THE FIELD FLOWER.

LEMOINE.

A SUNBROWN maid, a wild field flower,
　Once loved a wealthy yeoman's son ;
The poor haymaker had no dower,
　But the rich heart her lover won.
And as she wept the father spake
　One day, ' Come, mow this field of mine ;
If in three days is won the stake,
　Then in three days my son is thine.'

A sweet and tender tale I sing,
　Of love and grief a simple lay,
A touching half-forgotten thing
　The mowers tell among the hay.

The fond maid listened, and half thought
   Of love and joy to die outright ;
And in her hand her scythe she caught,
   And sore she laboured day and night ;
Fainting and well nigh in despair,
   Fresh power she sought from heaven above,
Her love new strength still won from prayer,
   And all her simple prayer was love.

A sweet and tender tale I sing,
   Of love and grief a simple lay,
A touching half-forgotten thing
   The mowers tell among the hay.

Once as she toiled, her yearning eye
   Fell on a little daisy near :
'Poor simple flower, must thou too die,
   For my true heart to win my Dear?'
But as beneath her scythe it fell,
   Its eye had such a pleading power,
Her breast must needs with pity swell—
   Was she not too a poor field flower?

A sweet and touching tale I sing,
   Of love and grief a simple lay,
A touching half-forgotten thing
   The mowers tell among the hay.

The third day duly to the vale
   Again the wealthy yeoman came ;
Breathless she was and deathly pale,
   But her young eyes with rapture flame.
' My girl, I did but jest,' he said,
   ' Here, these ten crowns your toil will pay.'
And by her scythe that eve lay dead
   One flower the more among the hay.

Such is the sweet and touching tale
   The mowers tell among the hay ;
And every maid within the vale
   Weeps as she sings that simple lay.

THE FOLDED LEAF.

' Love from his treasure bringeth forth things new and old.'
From the Persian.

It was a quiet place of leaves that took
    Religious meanings from her still-lit face,
    And set her beauty in a tender grace,
And voiceless sanctities about her shook.

Outstretched we lay and read in summer calm,
    Her cheek's most perfect curve, more smoothly pale
    Than nested throstles' eggs within the vale,
Cupped in the hollow of her rosy palm.

And from the passionate sad lay we read,
    A light struck up from love's fair rhythmic flow,
    That played about her lips, and touched her brow,
Like dancing light from water upward shed.

Breathless we read, till on two leaves we came
   Close shut as wings of poisèd butterflies,
   Hoarding their sun-loved jewels from all eyes,
Where Love in fire hath writ his secret name ;

Then all her brows' fair smoothness fretted grew,
   With little eager airs of baffled thought,
   And as to loose the page she something sought,
The silver dagger from her hair she drew.

When lo, her swathèd wealth of tresses rare
   About the page came tumbling all unwrought ;
   And all the glory of the poet's thought
Was blurred with golden glories of her hair.

But as she turned her face with queenly air,
   To wreathe the fragrant cloud about her head,
   I leant across the passion of the Dead,
And trembling kissed the perfect lips laid bare.

And so between the folded leaves, ah bliss !
   We found four sweeter leaves that closer clung,
   And parting, all that hopeless passion sung
Had found its consummation in a kiss.

THE EARRING.

I PIERCED her tender ear, shell-white,
　　With sharp hot pangs of words, I hurt
　　Her maiden pride with wild abuse,
I called her heartless, cruel, flirt—
　　Love that for very love must bruise
The gentle flower of his delight.

Across the angry breakers flung,
　　The voice of her heart's lord she heard,
　　And trembling on my breast she laid
The small gold head without a word ;
　　And in the wound my passion made,
The deep-sea pearl of love I hung.

WEDDED SLEEP.

DEEP in the quiet night they lay,
Shut in the eyeless dark away,
   Two hearts that, beating, one time keep,
   Each in a separate world of sleep.

Dreams came to them, dreams whispering low,
Dreams of each other long ago,
   As to their cotes come harmless doves ;
   And the quaint story of their loves,

Beneath forgotten morning skies,
Rose like a tree before their eyes,
   That in some trim old garden spreads,
   And leisurely its warm fruits sheds.

Again they watch it wild with fear,
Wild with sweet hopes and anguish dear
  The storm is in its boughs again,
  Its apple blossom weeps with rain.

Again the sudden sun breaks out,
The glad birds sing, the cuckoos shout,
  And winds that breathe their fond desires
  Do shake the rain-drops' hidden fires.

But as red-lipped the ripe fruit grows,
And each in happy stealth arose,
  To pluck its wealth beneath the sun—
  Love laughing tossed their worlds in one,

And Sleep soft slipped her veil away,
When lo, sweet mouth to mouth they lay ;
  And in the glimmering orchard near,
  The earliest bird sang loud and clear.

THE THUNDER SHOWER.

Up from the south a great cloud drew,
Trailing her dusky purples came
O'er the burning west, and sun-blanch'd blue ;
And her shadowy fingers deadening laid
On the throbbing chords of light that rayed
The deep horizons faint with flame.

O air-born daughter of the south,
O nursing mother of May flowers,
Bending to every thirsty mouth,
That drinks thy sweetness in secret bowers,
And wet-lipped sleeps to the hushing sound
Of thine infinite whispers of love around ;
Thou comest to us from over the sea,
Where my sailor boy is thinking of me ;
What dost thou bring from over the sea ?

K

An orient pearl for every flower,
And loosening silver for the leaves ;
Cool whispers rippling round the eaves,
And soft sweet pipings by the hour,
Of chilly birds in dim wet lanes,
And glades all haunted with grey rains,
And footfalls of the falling shower ;
And mellow thunders far away
From purple hollows dim with heat.
And for the dusty browning street
A smell of rain, with patches grey
Beneath the pelted chestnut bloom,
Where children gather from their play,
And passers-by a moment stay
To drink in all the cool perfume ;
For my loved one's grave a greening shower,
For my little sick child a cool soft sleep ;
And for these eyes that could not weep,
Heavy and dull as the passing hour,
   Waters divine that weep away
   The aching sweetness of a day,
   That has passed for ever and ever away.

ME IN THEE.

FROM THE PERSIAN.

ONE unto his Belovèd came,
And knocked and called upon her name ;
And from within a voice, full-sweet,
That made his heart to music beat,
 Cried, ' Who is there ? '
 And low he made reply,
  ' Love, it is I.'
But the voice spake in chill despair,
' No room within this narrow hut
 For thee and me.'
 And lo, immutably
  The door was shut.

Then that sad lover fled away,
And wept and fasted night and day

In desert places, making prayer,
Nor saw the kindly face of men.
And after many days again
To the Belovèd's door he came,
And knocked and called upon her name ;
  And from within a voice thereto
    Cried, ' Who is there ? '
  And he, whom love had taught, replied,
    ' It is thyself.'   And lo,
The door was opened wide.

THE LOVER'S MAY-DAY SONG.

Now breaks the day, and with bright hand
　Unseals the cisterns of the dawn,
And floods with light the dusky lawn,
　　And all the glimmering land ;
　　And breaks my heart for thee.
　　　Ah, bid it break,
　　　For thy dear sake,
　　Break into light and ecstasy.

Now breaks sun-warmed the barren bough—
　A wintry rod that graceless grew
Unblessed by heaven's own sun and dew—
　　Breaks into blossom now,
　　And breaks my heart for thee.
　　　Ah, bid it break,
　　　For mine own sake,
　　Break into flower and fruit to be.

Now breaks the silence into song,
  Spring's wingèd angel now is here,
And raptures ring out far and near,
    Flouting sad winter's wrong ;
    And breaks my heart for thee.
      Ah, bid it break,
      For love's own sake,
Break into vows 'twixt thee and me.

THE MAIDEN'S SONG.

THROUGH THE MEADOWS TO THE SEA.

Sighing, sighing,
Ah, sweet south !
But sweeter far the balmy kisses
Of his mouth.

Flying, flying,
Ah, blithe bee !
But my heart tastes a honey never
Known to thee.

Singing, singing,
Ah, dear bird !
But deeper by his lightest whisper
I am stirred.

Swaying, swinging,
Ah, frail flower !
But more my heart sways to his wishes
Every hour.

Crying, crying,
Ah, sea-mew !
Mine is a rest thou vainly seekest,
Storm-proof, true.

Sighing, sighing,
Ah, sad sea !
Hadst thou a heart to love, for thee, too,
Rest would be.

'GOOD NIGHT AND GOOD DAY.'

WHEN Love's white star had dipt amid
　　Dark honeysuckles in the lane ;
And in the charmèd dark, close hid,
　　The nightingale poured forth her pain ;
When winking marigolds had shut
　　Their golden fringes to the light—
　　Heaven's starry world on world o'erhead,
　　Love's world on world within outspread—
Her hand in his she shyly put,
　　And in the porch they said 'Good night.'

And when with meeting steps they bruised
　　The earliest dews beneath their feet,
And love's delicious shame confused
　　Their gaze with consciousness too sweet,

That hid in feigned indifference,
    Yet dashed her cheek with rosy day,
    While all his thoughts stood up to sing
    His praise who made so sweet a thing ;
Then thrilled through every happy sense,
    He touched her hand and said ' Good day.'

But now so deep, so windless deep,
    Has sunk the sea of their content,
It hath no shore to break its sleep,
    Or loose it into ravishment ;
No silver reach of morning grey,
    No golden edge of fading light ;
    But hushed their heart as brooding bird,
    Their lips by no good wishes stirred ;
For by his side 'tis all ' good day,'
    And in his arms 'tis still ' good night.'

THE BURIED THORN.

Love, when thou art not kind,
A leafless May bush then I grow,
Hung with cold fog-drops ; every wind
Shrills thro' me, sifting up the snow,
And chatter all my branches bare.
　My singing birds are fled,
The frozen nest itself is dead,
　　My leaf is shed,
And all my flowery eyes struck blind.
The thorn, the thorn alone is there,
　Love, when thou art not kind.

Love, when thou art but kind,
The selfsame bush in spring I grow ;
My young leaves babble to the wind,
Into warm blossom bursts the snow,
And budded pearls do stud my bower.

And from my greening heart,
No more the songs of spring depart,
While swift wings dart
Sweet food for new-fledged hopes to find ;
And ah ! the thorn is lost in flower,
Love, when thou art but kind.

HÆMONY.

Among the rest a small unsightly root,
But of divine effect, he culled me out ;
The leaf was darkish, and had prickles on it,
But in another country, as he said,
Bore a bright golden flower, but not in this soil ; .
He called it Hæmony.—MILTON.

A LITTLE dust the summer breeze
   Had sifted up within a cleft,
A slanted raindrop from the trees,
   A tiny seed by chance airs left—
It was enough ; the seedling grew,
And from the barren rock-heart drew
Her dimpled leaf and tender bud,
And dews that did the bare rock stud ;
And crowned at length her simple head
With utter sweetness, breathed afar,

And burning like a dusky star—
　Sweetness upon so little fed,
　　Ah me ! ah me !
And yet hearts go uncomforted.

For hearts, dear Love, such seedlings are,
　That need so little, ah, so less
Than little on this earth, to bear
　The sun-sweet blossom, happiness ;
And sing—those dying hearts that come
To go—their swan-song flying home.
A touch, a tender tone—no more—
A face that lingers by the door
To turn and smile, a fond word said,
A kiss—these things make heaven ; and yet
We do neglect, refuse, forget,
To give that little, ere 'tis fled,
　　Ah me ! ah me !
And sad hearts go uncomforted.

I asked of thee but little, nay,
　Not for the golden fruit thy bough

Ripens for thee and thine who day
  By day beneath thy shadow grow ;
Only for what, from that full store,
Had made me rich, nor left thee poor,
A drift of blossom, needed not
For fruit, yet blessing some dim spot.
  A touch, a tender word soon said,
Fond tones that seem our Dead again
Come back after long years of pain,
    Lonely, for these my sick heart bled—
        Ah me ! ah me !
Sad hearts that go uncomforted.

LADY, WHY ART THOU SAD?

VICTOR HUGO.

LADY, why art thou sad amid delight,
     Why dost thou weep forlorn?
Lovely of soul but mournful as the night,
     Thou, fair as summer morn.

What recks it that this fickle life unjust
     To man and maid below,
Beneath thy feet still crumbles into dust?
     Thy deathless spirit know!

Thy soul that soon perchance will take her flight
     To some pure clime afar,
And bear thee far above our dolorous night,
     Beyond our fret and jar.

Be like the bird that rests one moment long
    On boughs too weak to bear,
Feels the branch bend, nor stays her happy song,
    Conscious her wings are there.

'Je mourrai seul.'—*Pascal*.

THE silent chariot standeth at the door,
The house is hushed and still from roof to floor,
None heard the sound of its mysterious wheels,
    Yet each its presence feels.

No champing bit, nor tramp of pawing feet,
All dark and silent up and down the street,
And yet thou may'st not keep it waiting there
    For one last kiss or prayer.

Thy words, with some strange Other interchanged,
Strike cold across us like loved eyes estranged,
With things that are not fraught ; our things that are
    Fade like a sun-struck star.

And thou too weak and agonised to lift
The cup to quench thy dying thirst, or shift

Thy pillow, now without our help must rise,
      Nor wait our ministries.

Thou, loved and cherished, must go forth alone,
None sees thee fondly to the door, not one ;
No head is turned to see thee go ; we stay
      Where thou art not, and pray.

No panel bars thy white resistless feet,
Our walls are mist to thee ; out in the street
It waits, It waits for thee, for thee alone :
      ' Arise, let us begone.'

Alone, alone upon thine awful way !
Do any show thee kindness ?   Any stay
Thy heart ?   Or does the silent charioteer
      Whisper ' Be of good cheer ' ?

We know not.   None may follow thee afar,
None hear the sound of thy departing car.
Only vast silence like a strong black sea
      Rolls in 'twixt us and thee.

THE TWO WORLDS.

Two mighty silences, two worlds unseen
   Over against each other lie ;
For ever boundlessly apart have been,
     For ever nigh.

In one is God Himself, and angels bright
   Do congregate, and spirits fair ;
And, lost to sight in depths of mystic light,
     Our Dead dwell there.

All things that cannot fade, nor fall, nor die,
   Voices beloved and precious things foregone,
Float up and up, and in that silence high
     With God grow one.

No barren silence, nay, but such as over
   Lips that we love its spell may fling,

Where tender words like nested swallows hover,
    Ere they take wing.

Sometimes from that far land there comes a breeze,
    Soft airs surprise us on our way,
A dew drops from above ; then on our knees
    We fall and pray.

And oft in some low crimson coast of cloud
    We deem we see its far-off strand ;
Our hearts like shipwrecked sailors cry aloud,
    'The land ! The land !'

And side by side that other world unknown,
    Drenched in unbroken silence lies—
World of ourselves, where each one lives alone,
    And lonely dies.

With our unuttered griefs, our joys untold,
    Our multitudinous thoughts' swift throng
We dwell ; one silence them and us doth fold
    All our life long.

Out from those depths there comes a cry of pain,
'Ah, pitifully, Lord,' it calls,
'Behold the sorrows of our hearts!' and then—
A silence falls.

Die down, die down, O thou tormented sea!
Suffer my silent world to fill
With voices from that land which call to me,
'We love thee still.'

In vain—I hear them not; but o'er my loss
Comes an apocalyptic voice:
'There shall be no more sea, and thou canst cross.'
Rejoice! Rejoice!

COR CORDIUM.

Sweet soul, the world is loud against thy name,
  In righteous wrath men shut thee from their doors,
And women's kindly looks, deep-fraught with blame,
  Fold up their tender hues like chilly flowers
Before the storm, whene'er thy name is heard,
  Nor yield thee charity of smile nor word.

But I ne'er think of thee, nor pray, nor dream,
  But in these eyes, that sadly scanned thy face,
Waters divine well up from some far stream
  That hath its rise in some dear land of grace
Far hence, where Love and Pity, tenderer grown,
  Have wept and kissed their sweet selves into one.

For still I feel thee pure, though wild thy word,
   And marred thy thought, and all unsweet thy creed :
And like a wayside Christ thou standest, blurred,
   Disfeatured, blank with storm and wind and weed,
The dear divinity of look all fled,
   But still the tender pleading arms outspread.

Thou wert to me like some fine instrument
   Of music wrought from a fair forest tree,
That choral grew to morning winds, and lent
   A leafy tongue to all soft airs that be ;
Or dimly massed against the evening sky,
   Breathless in moon-enchanted dreams did lie.

For thou wert one with Nature ; unto thee
   Her thought grew vocal to the sense within
That penetrates her voiceless mystery ;
   And thine were incantations strong to win
Fair harmony from mute indifferent things,
   And wake the hidden life that soars and sings.

But when the world's great wrong, its curse and pain,
　　Clutched at thy trembling chords, thy spirit pure,
Attuned to winds, still lights, and falling rain,
　　Finding no resolution sweet, no sure
Accord, no voice of hope, no upward glow,
　　Broke with that incommunicable woe.

And now thine ancient melodies are fled ;
　　The young dews weep but o'er fair woman lost,
The lark is cruel, a careless god o'erhead
　　That sings his fill when hearts are breaking most ;
The lily wears her festive white forlorn,
　　The rose's odorous breath is all forsworn.

No truth, no faith, no purity of will
　　Thou seest anywhere, 'tis discord all ;
And evermore thou hear'st the underswell
　　Of human sin, and woe, and passion's thrall ;
Thy old sweet uses homeless sob in pain
　　About thy riven chords in vain, in vain !

O unstrung Heart and Will ! the dolorous blast
  That passing broke thy music into pain,
Pours through the mighty organ-pipes at last,
  And all the loveless roar that vexed thy brain
Storms into music jubilant and calm,
  And thunders through the worlds a victor's psalm.

THE MYSTERY OF PAIN.

'ʼTis but a little boon, O friends ! I crave,
Will He not, think you, hear my heart's last cry ?
The thunder of His power is shown to save,
Will He not surely grant it ere I die ?'

With pitying hands we smoothed the tortured brow,
Turned not from those sad pleading eyes away ;
For him we would have laid the dear life low,
And measuring love by love, we answered 'Yea.'

He lay there in his strength, no more to rise,
Like some great bough, rent by a sudden gust,
Full-blossomed, all its leafy melodies,
And singing birds laid silent in the dust.

And yet not so ; earth on her painless brow
Ne'er wore that agony of human thought,

That of before and after makes its woe,
By memory filled, from saddening forethought caught.

Earth's tender things came to him dying there ;
The vast and pitying air of heaven blew in,
Parting with dewy touch the fevered hair ;
The cuckoo's note from distant groves came thin ;

The morn's first tender chirpings round the eaves
Told him the night was gone, her phantoms laid ;
The showery shiver of cool aspen leaves
Lulled him, but could not grant him what he prayed.

And still with that pathetic voice that took
Lorn echoes from the subterranean caves
Of human pain, he asked, with wistful look,
' Will He not grant me what my spirit craves ? '

Could we then say him nay, or meet in vain
Those dark eyes' pleading power—sad eyes where lay
Death's shadow heavy as a sleep—nor feign
The soothing smile, and answer ' Surely yea ? '

And yet he died without it, lingering,
With that sad asking cadence in his tone,
Like that unfinished note with which, in spring,
The shy wood-pigeon mourns in woodlands lone.

What was it then on which his heart was set?
A little space free from pain's maddening power,
One little hour for love and prayer ; and yet
He died in agony, nor saw that hour.

O Love ! we cannot understand nor hear
The voice thou speakest in—we know not whence ;
Its octave is too vast for human ear,
And sounds blank silence to the listening sense.

Thou hast eternity to love in, Thee
Time urges not ; in thine eternal years
Thy large plan ripens to a whole, while we
Must love in haste betwixt life's smiles and tears.

Thou Who didst know all storms that waste the heart,
Thou Who didst drain our woe, nor taste our balm ;

Thou saw'st the whole, where we but see the part—
Doubting we turn to Thee, and Thou art calm.

All cries of pain, all precious hopes foregone,
All mysteries of regent ill, all balm
Asked but denied, solution vast, unknown,
Find in that even brow's triumphant calm.

And as a child who fears some stranger's gaze,
Wraps itself, clinging to its mother's side,
Within her robe, nor sees its mother's face,
But knows her near, and so is satisfied;

So from our life's dread mystery, O Lord,
Within thy bounteous vesture's hem we hide ;
And brave all sights of ill, and wait thy word,
When knowing all we shall be satisfied.

1868.

A DIRGE.

Sleep, sweetheart, sleep !
Fold the green about thee close ;
Shrillest cry that ever rose,
Wail of world-old wrongs and woes
Railings of thy bitter foes,
Shatter not thy deep repose.
Sleep, sweetheart, sleep !

Sleep, sweetheart, sleep !
Thou didst sink in thickest night,
Thou to all in gloom a light,
Thou whose passion was the right,
Thou a wonder and delight,
Sank without a star in sight.
Sleep, sweetheart, sleep !

Sleep, sweetheart, sleep !
Lift thy darkened eyes, behold,
Winking lights of spring unfold,
Starry watch about thee hold,
Daisies pied and crocus gold,
Flame the myriad blades untold.
Sleep, sweetheart, sleep !

Sleep, sweetheart, sleep !
Wring thy tender hands no more,
Hands thy loved ones once forswore,
Deemed them foul and stained with gore,
Since old lies to earth they tore,
Hands that every burthen bore.
Sleep, sweetheart, sleep !

Sleep, sweetheart, sleep !
We were cruel, pierced thee, smote ;
Now but tender wing'd things float
In the low sun, mote on mote,
Shrill to thee their humble note ;
Honey-bees upon thee doat,

Sea-sighs come to thee afloat.
    Sleep, sweetheart, sleep !

    Sleep, sweetheart, sleep !
Nay, what ailed thee still to groan,
Feel the world's wrong as thine own ?
Couldst thou not dance to woman's moan,
Eat and drink and pipe it down,
Wiser with the wise world grown ?
    Sleep, sweetheart, sleep !

    Sleep, sweetheart, sleep !
Thou didst dash thyself in vain
'Gainst old wrongs, nor shook their reign ;
Couldst not lift the weight of pain
Off man's heart that writhes again,
Wert but crushed thyself and slain.
    Sleep, sweetheart, sleep !

    Sleep, sweetheart, sleep
Nature guards thy sacred grief,
Night-winds sigh it in the leaf,

M

Throstles give it sweet relief,

Billows in a foamy sheaf

Thunder it against the reef.

    Sleep, sweetheart, sleep !

    Sleep, sweetheart, sleep !

From thy grave a blade we take,

In thy heart's blood dip and slake,

Thus a sword of God we make,

Stoutest wrongs can never break .

Steel grow grass blades for thy sake.

    Sleep, sweetheart, sleep !

    Sleep, sweetheart, sleep !

In thy failure strong we grow ;

Flung in passion on the foe,

Count we not the serried row ;

For the Dead baptisèd now,

Dare to fail, and conquer so.

    Sleep, sweetheart, sleep !

THE SWORD OF GOD.

An angel went forth with the kingdoms of darkness
    to war.
Not from the Infinite came he, not from afar,
For the immutable world, the eternal is here.
Earth and the sea, and the stars, and the voices I
    hear,
Are but its glory as veiled to the sense and the sight,
Shapings and shadowings of the ineffable light ;
The infinite Word of God that filleth all space
Broken on infant lips into tenderest grace.

He came not, he was, slowly gathering out of the light
Into majestic shape on my awe-stricken sight,
As a thunder-cloud gathers in August, we know not
    from whence,
Out of the paling blue of the heat, on the sense ;

And the sweep of his purple is heard in the sultry
      leaves,
And the hot parch'd earth at his coming a long sigh
      heaves—
Merciful and mighty, so he arose on the world,
Seeking a weapon to fight hell's forces uphurled.

O earth ! earth ! earth ! what sword wilt thou give to
      his ire,
Welded and wrought of the fierceness of terrible fire,
Baptised in keen ice that splits the granite in twain,
Whose lightnings flicker swift death on the fierce
      battle plain,
To utter the might of his arm laid bare against wrong?
What earthly weapon of temper so keen and so
      strong
As to hold the rush of his soul in battle, what sword
The rapture of anger angelic, the wrath of the Lord?

When lo, he paused by my garden—a slow, deep
      smile
Made an awful light about his mute lips the while,

As he gathered a tall white lily that trembled and
    bowed;

And pity fainted within me, crying aloud :

'Not that, oh my lord, not that ! such a tender thing,

Made but for cool soft touches of dews at day spring,

Made to dream out its days in festival white and
    gold,

To gossip with bees and all love's sweetness unfold.'

But he passed, nor heard my pitiful human wail,

And his face was set to the battle wrathfully pale ;

Behind him his vesture streamed out from his dread
    glancing form,

As streams the long foam from the back of the billow
    in storm,

One arm held before him to scatter the smoke of his
    foes,

The stench of man's evil, the reek of his fathomless
    woes ;

With the other outstretched he smote to the left and
    the right,

With the lily he bore in his hand, the sword of his might.

And wherever the lily fell the darkness was scattered,

And wherever the lily smote the evil was shattered;

Tyrannous force with the strength of the granite but
now

Crumbled to churchyard dust at a touch, scarce a
blow,

Of that weakness divine, that whiteness caught from
the dawn,

And dungeons of hate to their deep foundations yawn,

And out of the stricken stones mild waters gush forth,

Rivers of God that flow to the south from the north.

And still men cursed at the lily and hacked it and
tore,

And some it smote on their knees to pray once more,

And some smote down on their faces, biting the dust,

And clamour and groans, brave love and bloodiest lust;

Till a sudden song like a burst of thrushes at dawn,

Told the battle was won, the forces of evil withdrawn;

And I knew that one more deliverance was wrought
on the earth,

' Glory to God ' men sang in jubilant mirth.

But the lily, my lily that showed so gracious that
morn ;

Ah me, all battered and wrung and faded and torn,

Never again to walk in innocent white,

Her virginal snows all smirched with the reek of the
fight ;

The sweat of man's anguish where once lay the dew
and the rain,

Her golden heart bruised and torn with utterest pain.

And I wept for my lily ; and still, as I wept on apart,

I seemed to be weeping and weeping a woman's heart.

A VISION OF WOMANHOOD.

OUT in the desert, half-submerged, a sphinx
Gazed at her awful mirrored loveliness,
In dull deep waters sunk of Lethe, fed
By the dark river of the unknown source ;
Gazed at the pure high face that answered hers,
As moon to moon, and lovely moulded curves
Of motherhood that shaped the pure white breast,
And deemed she saw herself, nor knew
That just below the shining surfaces
The woman sickened into unclean beast,
Bestial, with ravening claws and murderous strength ;
And all around were strewn the bones of men,
And eyeless sockets filled with desert dust
Of those who cursed her with a dying curse.

Then a great Angel, standing in the sun,
Smote those dull Lethe-waters and they fled,
And all her hidden shame to her lay bare ;
And in her agony she knew herself
To be half woman and half beast unclean,
That grew to her and made one shuddering flesh
With her, inextricably one with death.
And all her being burned as in a furnace,
And the cold stone was fused about her heart
Into warm blood and sweat of agony ;
While men awe-stricken gazed upon her woe,
And every kingdom wailed because of her,
And all the land was darkened for her sake.
Then as one dead before her feet I fell,
Made one with her intolerable shame.

Æons or hours did that deep trance endure ?
When the dark veil of that abysmal sleep
Was rent in twain by a loud trumpet sound,
And starting up, I saw a temple vast,
And many worshippers therein were bowed.
But on the upturned faces, I beheld

The light of a new world, and homage high,

As that a queen may render to her king,

Who owning a subjection yet remains

A majesty—such pure manhood on them lay.

And high above all worshippers enthroned,

Lo, the Egyptian woman who abode

With Death in desert places ; and behold

The beast was slain, the deathful riddle solved

That slew the man ; and throned upon men's hearts—

A wall of fire to guard her round about—

A perfect woman in her weakness rose,

And in her arms the future's child divine.

THE WORLD'S OUTCASTS.

Down the world's great highway driven,
  Roof and wall and sun-sick street
All aflame with dreadful faces,
  That upon Him glare and beat,
And a roar of awful voices—
  Hissed and hooted, cursed and stoned,
Lo, He passeth, He the outcast,
    Man-disowned.

Then a shout of coarse derision,
  And the seething, surging crowd
Stop and thicken into silence,
  Round some central object bowed ;
Where, beneath His shameful burthen
  And a woe too deep to trace,
Dumbly He hath fallen forward
    On His face.

Who is poor enough and abject
   To help lift the shameful weight ?
Who so lost and cursed already
   As to share His meed of hate ?
Bear with Him a world's derision,
   He, the world's great castaway,
Made supreme with Him in anguish
   Where He lay.

Only two in all the people—
   One a slave with bruisèd flesh ;
And a lost girl from the country,
   Caught in pleasure's spangled mesh,
Once all white with virginal blossom,
   Now befouled, cast off, decried—
These they drave with cruel laughter
   To His side.

And on them they laid the burthen,
   But for such as these too vile,
Heeding not his lash-torn shoulders
   As on him the load they pile ;

Heeding not the cruel bruising
  Of that girlish flesh of hers,
As the vast procession slowly
    Onward stirs.

Ever down the world's great highways
  To the faithful tear-washed eye,
Moves that sad and strange procession ;
  Ever on their way to die,
Signing evil with their life-blood,
  Marking for the axe, the tree,
With the Holy, the degraded,
    One in three.

Not in vain ye bear His burthen,
  Slaves, whose groaning no man hears,
God's great image charred and blackened ;
  Lost ones, weeping bitter tears,
By man's lust to shame devoted,
  Fouled your womanhood's sacred springs,
He walks with you, He, the Outcast,
    King of kings.

God's elect to sore destruction,
　　Cursed and smitten for man's sin !
Through your bloody sweat and anguish
　　Higher life for man ye win ;
Yea, for very shame and pity
　　He shall rise by your deep fall,
Know by some remorseful passion
　　Love is all.

RUBÁIYÁT.

Ever from less to more the purpose runs,
That threads in one vast light a myriad suns,
   A music in so vast an octave set
That oft its thunder into silence stuns.

The perfect circle of eternity
In time is but a crooked line to thee.
   Wait, and the sun-bow's jewelled curve behold,
Wait, and Love's perfect orbit thou shalt see.

Deem not Love works in time ; his work is one;
Beginning, end, exists in thee alone ;
   But since his full-orb'd thought would strike thee
     dead,
With burning ecstasies of light foredone,

For thee his glory into days he breaks,
And days he crumbles into stars, and makes
    His light successive pass before thine eyes,
His purpose broken small thy wonder wakes.

Love orders all ; with ordered steps and fair
Each leaf climbs up its jewelled winding stair ; [2]
    The stars in golden rhythms rise and set,
His words are music to the eye and ear.

But lest his harmonies too constant flow
For the created sense to hear or know,
    He breaks them into discords, which in turn
Beneath his hand to vaster music grow.

To speak, all things their opposites must meet,
Honey must in the bitter find her sweet ;
    Silence forswear herself in sound, ere known,
The light be slain of dark to grow complete.

And Love, to know himself as Love indeed,
Must not his fulness wed with utter need ;
    The Life indeed still find himself in death,
His deepest word be pain and things that bleed ?

[2] *See* Note.

The word must die, the deathless meaning lives,
Silence enriched by all sad music gives,
　The life laid down retaken glorified,
Love's mystic spiral that still upward strives.

For still in spirals vast move life and love,
In lines upon themselves returning move,
　Evil that good defeats, but in its turn
Made vaster good that higher climbs above.

Ever from less to more his purpose grows,
Ever a life becoming, till the rose
　Of Love supreme, his thought's consummate flower,
At length will crown the age's toil and woes ;

And show all things are made to play his part,
Death gives his crown, the lightning's crooked dart
　He straightens to the sceptre of his power,
Worlds rise and set to beatings of his Heart.

LIFE'S COST.

I COULD not at the first be born
But through another's bitter wailing pain ;
Another's loss must be my sweetest gain,
And love, only to win that I might be,
    Must wet her couch forlorn
With tears of blood and sweat of agony.

Since then I cannot live a week,
But some fair thing must leave the daisied dells,
The joy of pastures, bubbling springs and wells,
And grassy murmurs of its peaceful days,
    To bleed in pain, and reek,
And die, for me to tread life's pleasant ways.

I cannot, sure, be warmed or lit,
But men must crouch and toil in tortuous caves
Bowed on themselves, while day and night in waves
Of blackness wash away their sunless lives ;
　　　Or blasted and sore hit,
　　Dark life to darker death the miner drives.

Naked, I cannot clothed be,
But worms must patient weave their satin shroud,
The sheep must shiver to the April cloud,
Yielding his one white coat to keep me warm ;
　　　In shop and factory
　　For me must weary toiling millions swarm.

With gems I deck not brow or hands,
But through the roaring dark of cruel seas
Some wretch, with shuddering breath and trembling
　　　knees,
Goes headlong, while the sea-sharks dodge his quest :
　　　Then at my door he stands,
　　Naked, with bleeding ears and heaving chest.

I fall not on my knees and pray,
But God must come from heaven to fetch that sigh,
And piercèd Hands must bear it back on high ;
And through His broken heart and cloven side
　　　Love makes an open way
　　For me, who could not live but that He died.

　　O awful sweetest life of mine,
That God and man both serve in blood and tears !
O prayers I breathe not but through other prayers !
O breath of life, compact of others' sighs !
　　　With this dread gift divine,
　　Ah ! whither go, what worthily devise ?

　　If on myself I dare to spend
This dreadful thing, in pleasure lapped and reared,
What am I but a hideous idol smeared
With human blood, that with its carven smile,
　　　Alike to foe and friend,
　　Maddens the wretch who perishes the while ?

I will away and find my God,

And what I dare not keep, ask Him to take,

And, taking, Love's sweet sacrifice to make.

Then, like a wave, the sorrow and the pain

High heaven with glory flood ;

For me, for them, for all, a splendid gain.

THE SOUL'S MYSTERY.

I saw a mighty Angel stand,
    Fronting the sun, upon the earth.
Something he held within his hand,
I knew not what ; when that dark unknown birth
Into the fire remorselessly he cast ;
        And there went up the smoke
Of its great torment through the land,
    Nor pity in the Angel woke.
And unto him I cried aghast :
        ' Ah, lord, what doest thou ? '
When lo ! from out the ashes of the brand
    A lily rose with golden heart aglow,
Wet with cool dews, no smell of fire at all
Upon her garments white and virginal.

But that dread Angel, pausing not,
    Thrust in his hand, and rudely tore
The lily from its fragrant plot,
And all disrooted flung it from the shore
Into deep whelming waters for its shroud ;
      And as it sank there rose
    Infinite sobbings of the sea,
    And hollow sound of many woes.
And unto him I cried aloud :
      ' Ah, lord, what doest thou? '
When at his feet the waves washed up in glee
    A perfect pearl, that like a star did glow,
The lily's whiteness hardened to a gem,
Fit glory for a kingly diadem.

But he who knew no human ruth,
    Took that fair preciousness in trust,
    Then, wanton, with a stone's sharp tooth,
Fretted and ground it into worthless dust ;
And whirling dust grew all the stars on high,
      Dust for its sake the world,
And empty dust the lifeless All

Through vacant spaces onward hurled.
And like a wail arose my cry:
    ' Ah, lord, what doest thou ? '
When lo ! a perfect star, more virginal
Than that fair lily, with a brighter glow
Than sea-washed pearl, a splendour on its throne,
Eternal in the heavens above me shone.

And musing on the mystic whole,
I knew it for a human soul ;
Through love, through pain, through death at bitter
    strife,
The power attaining of an endless life.

THE REVIVALISTS.

'WHAT think you of these preachers? Mountebanks
Methinks, whose trick it is to draw the crowd ;
With their fanatic talk of hell unfit
For cultured men, their utterance uncouth,
Their narrow creed, and broad vulgarity.
'Tis but a passing stir, a blaze of straw,
That scarce will leave an empty ash behind it.'

That night I had a vision in the dark.
It was a picture wrought by some dead hand
In days when men in such a glory walked,
Their thoughts cast mighty shadows on the wall.
Right in the centre, fronting, stood the Christ,
In faded vesture clad, a toil-worn Man,
With labour-hardened palms, not beautiful,
But for the sad divinity of look,

And the divine compassions mutely rained
From down-dropt eyes, and slow deep-smiling lips
On one which was a sinner at His feet,
Her arms flung out in infinite appeal
From man that cursed, to God who does but bless
One sad cheek pillowed softly on the foot
That pausing waits, not to disturb her there.
And by her kneels an older woman, one,
Grown old in sin and sorrow not her own—
Haply some loved one's—while one pendant hand
Just sweeps the prostrate figure at her side,
The other closely clasps the Christ's strong hand,
Her eyes uplifted with that far-away
Worshipping look of one who now has found
A heart in which to lay her lost, a home
To lay her anguish down.   But on the right
A little child has wrapped the Saviour's robe
About itself, and from its hiding-place
Peers out with bright uncomprehending eyes,
While on the curly head His hand is laid.
And further still, a working man with tools
Upon his back, pausing, surveys the scene,

With pondering looks in meditation lost.
But on the left full in the foreground stand
Two Greeks, in robes of feasting, crowned with flowers,
Fresh from some bright procession of the gods,
Music and dance, and glorious poesy,
A little drawn to one another stand,
And, gazing half averted, criticise
The scene—the sordid clothes, the womanhood
That fouls the passing thought, the street display—
With curling lip and air of fine disgust !

And, gazing on that masterpiece, I cried,
' Let not fine culture, poesy, art, sweet tones,
Build up about my soothèd sense a world
That is not Thine, and wall me up in dreams ;
So my sad heart may cease to pulse with Thine,
The great World-Heart, whose blood, for ever shed
Is human life, whose ache is man's dumb pain.
Let not my grasp on Life's most awful Truth
Be loosened ; but where'er the people hear,
Quick-eared, as closer unto life, Thy step,
And thronging bring their dumb hearts unto Thee,

To ease the ache that has no easeful words,

There, through all rudest speech and gestures mean,

Obscuring sights, and harsh fanatic sounds,

Still may I see the Christ in faded vesture ;

Nor stand with Greeks and coldly criticise

The mean apparel, in whose tarnished hem,

By a diviner instinct led, the lost,

The sad, the poor, the sinful find sweet healing,

But with that outcast woman in the dust,

Heart of our hearts ! may worship and adore.

LIFE'S ISSUES.

A CARELESS step and that was all.
    Thy heedless foot
Passed on, no cloud did o'er thee fall,
And yet behind thee where it prest,
    A broken blossom dying lay,
Crushed in the dust its silver crest.
    And now no more, at dawn of day,
Its simple star in that low plot
    Will rise, or rosy set at even ;
And earth has one more barren spot,
    Touched with no starry thought of heaven,
For evermore a darkened joy,
A happiness thou didst destroy,
    O heedless foot !

A careless moment, that was all.
   Thine idle hand
On a fair thing of life did fall,
Then thou didst wander on at ease.
   But it lay there and writhed in pain,
No more to mount upon the breeze
   Nor poise in dewy shades again
A palpitating light of wings,
   That now dust-dim can only creep ;
And hushed the tender murmurings
   That sang the honeyed buds to sleep
For evermore a darkened joy,
A happiness thou didst destroy,
      O idle hand !

A careless mood, yes, that was all.
   With heedless heart,
Thou didst pass on and hear no call,
And yet, close to thy careless talk,
   A heart lay drowning in despair,
Waiting the word to rise and walk ;
   A heart to whom one word or prayer

Of thine, had been the touch of Christ,
  Telling that unseen Love was near ;
But failing which, in storm and mist,
  It sank, while thou went'st soft and fair,
For evermore a darkened joy,
A happiness thou didst destroy,
    O heedless heart !

Child of high heaven and hell beneath,
    O man, beware !
In mysteries of life and death,
Of joy, despair, thy feet are set ;
  All things are big with suffering,
And in thy lightest act are met,
  And prisoned up on folded wing,
Gigantic forces, good or ill,
  Which way thou lett'st them loose at last.
O walk in prayer, be tender still,
  And reverent move, lest from the past
Rise as thy curse some darkened joy,
Some happiness thou didst destroy,
    O man, beware !

FAILURE.

ART thou nigh beaten in the battle dread,
Beaten down on thy knee, and sore bestead?
    Then on thy knee
Beneath the stars to the great whole upsoar,
In dust and darkness worship and adore.

Is thy sword shivered in thy helpless hands,
Smiting the wrong that still thy force withstands?
    Then in thy heart,
Thy fainting heart, the splinters hide, that so
Thy blood may richer for the world's life flow.

Dost thou weep bitter tears o'er hopes foregone,
O'er ills unrighted, faith belied, undone?
    Arise, praise God!
Who gives thee deep-sea pearls of priceless worth,
To diadem the right discrowned on earth.

Are all thine efforts fruitless, vain, ill-sped,
Futile and weak as broken ends of thread?
    Yea, even so!
Of broken shells He maketh, so He wills,
The everlasting marble of His hills.

'Evil is all too strong,' dost fainting cry?
'It conquers life and labour, let me die!'
    Yet ere thou die,
Show thou the stronger: good that conquers death,
Failing, grows strong, struck down, but wins new
      breath.

Out of the tumbling deeps comes thy last cry,
'There is no God, what good to toil and die?'
    Go to, faint heart!
Strike from the dark the light that proves the Light,
No God? Create Him, dying for the right!

ABSOLVO TE.

I.

I MADE an idol secretly,
And hugged and kissed it in the dark,
  And let my life blood run to waste ;
Until, all wan and faint, I rose in haste,
And in the fire, hoping that none would mark,
Remorseful cast my hugg'd impiety ;
  And in her rosy palms, the flame
A moment darkening, caught my hidden shame,
Then into molten jewels wrought it bright,
And made it into upward-springing light,
  While fell a fluttering sigh from heaven
    'Go, sin no more,
      Thou art forgiven.'

II.

I fouled my garments, walking fast
And furious in forbidden ways ;
   Then shame-struck plunged them in a spring,
That of the stainless blue ran murmuring ;
And all her limpid soul in dim amaze,
Her azure heavens put out, grew overcast ;
   But brightening soon, she washed the stain
Away, and left my garments white again ;
Then, all absolving, spread her beamy net,
And bade her blue Forget-me-nots forget,
   While came a murmur soft from heaven :
         'Go, sin no more,
         Thou art forgiven.'

III.

I spake in bitter hate one day,
And jangling beat a jarring chord,
   Nor would have done for any man ;
But the mild air nimbly my wrath outran,

And from my lips washed off the bitter word,

Washed with a smell of balm and dews away ;

   And o'er the jarring place she shook,

Her nearest skylark's song in mild rebuke,

And her torn silence healed with hum of bees,

From the next woodbine murmuring at ease ;

   Then breathed in leafy sighs from heaven :

      'Go, sin no more,

      Thou art forgiven.'

IV.

   I wrought a foulness on the earth,

Then sickening with its evil breath,

   Thrust the dead carcase in the ground,

Lest any saw me peering furtive round ;

But the earth mildly hid it up beneath

Her bosom's folds, and at her springtime's birth,

   Of that foul rottenness below,

She made her apple-blossom's rosy snow,

And all her herbs that rooted from it grew,

Smelled but a goodly smell of rain and dew,

While her glad birds sang straight from heaven :
          ' Go, sin no more,
          Thou art forgiven.'

               v.

  Ah, wondrous blessed world of ours !
Ah, fountain opened evermore
  For all uncleanness ! minister
Of elemental love that everywhere
About me flows, and works in sea and shore,
In fire and air, with love's absolving powers.
  Oh let thy gentleness make me great,
That I may keep all day the simple state
Of thy pure springs, thy blowing clover, skies
Of morn and evening, stars, and odorous sighs ;
  Nor need again that voice from heaven :
          ' Go sin no more,
          Thou art forgiven.'

THE SUPREME KISS.

LIGHTLY we kissed and parted,
One kiss of many more to be ;
Nor once behind the kiss, light-hearted,
The moanings heard in thought
Of the irrevocable sea ;
Nor the light dippings caught
Of the inexorable oar
To waft thee to the undiscovered shore ;
Nor heard the ghostly wind of Nevermore
Shrill thro' the house and sob about the door :
Nor even in a dream—
So deep a sleep life sleeps,
Rocked on the everlasting deeps—
Felt the eternity
Roll in 'twixt thee and me,
That made that careless kiss supreme.

IN MY GARDEN.

WHAT shall I gather thee, Belovèd?
  What shall I gather thee?
    Roses, red roses,
    Roses for thee and me?
My cheek is pale, and thine is wan,
  And one is white and marble cold
As the cold stones 'tis pillowed on,
  While the great earth is onward rolled.
Our rose of morn is faded in the east,
  Our rose of life is overblown,
And drops in vacant sunsets down the west,
  Instinct with death and dear love flown
    Gather no roses,
No roses, Love, for thee and me.

What shall I gather thee, Belovèd?
　　What shall I gather thee?
　　　Lilies, white lilies,
　　　Lilies for thee and me?
Dead are the old white thoughts divine,
　　No golden dream shrined lily-wise
Lurks at thy saddened heart and mine,
　　No vision of the unspotted skies;
The outcast comes to sleep within thy breast,
　　And sounds of woe and sights of wrong
Have smirched our whiteness, while we fight
　　Foul ills on helpless blood grown strong.
　　　Gather no lilies,
No lilies, Love, for me and thee.

What shall I gather thee, Belovèd?
　　What shall I gather thee?
　　　Posies, sweet posies,
　　　But what for thee and me?
Primroses, wan as thine own smiles,
　　And like them dipped in sudden tears?
Violets, with subtle odorous wiles
　　To call back the departed years,

And pierce us with our heart's sad secrets told ?
   Daisies, our morning stars that set
At evening weeping ?   Daffodils, whose gold
   Redeems not Love, Death's thrall as yet ?
      Gather not any,
Nay, none of these for me and thee.

What shall I gather, say, Belovèd ?
   What shall I gather thee ?
    Blossoms, bright blossoms,
   Yet none for thee and me ?
Nay, but one flower beneath the light
   My garden keeps for us apart,
Dark as a moonless summer night,
   But with the day-star at her heart.
Still at our mortal touch her virtues die—
   I may not gather it, my sweet ;
But one of God's great angels passing by,
   One day shall pause, and at his feet
     Gather dark Heartsease,
   Heartsease, dear Love, for thee and me.

LOVE'S QUESTION AND ANSWER.

WHAT art thou, O my life ! now he is gone,
Now he is gone,
And left thee lone,
To smite sad-eyed the kindling morning skies,
Each day with death's dull ever-new surprise,
Now he is gone, thy dear one gone?
My life replies,
And plaining cries,
'Only a last year's acorn cup to hold
But empty rains that grasped the oak of old.'

What art thou, O my heart ! now he is gone,
Now he is gone,
Thy life, thine own,
Wronging all lovely things beneath the sky
That have no right to live now Love can die,
Now he is gone, thy dear one gone?

My heart replies,

My heart that dies,

' A little bird tossed from the nest, dead, dead,

I' the spring, while all the world sings overhead.'

What art thou, O my joy ! now he is gone,

Now he is gone,

And thou must moan,

Counting the tedious years that may not bring

His face, his voice, all empty of the spring,

Now he is gone, thy dear one gone ?

My joy replies,

And farewell sighs,

' A little star that fadeth from its place

In a departed glow, and leaves no trace.'

What art thou, O my hope ! now he is gone

Now he is gone

A way unknown,

Across a silent sea, unlit by sail,

Unswept by wing, or thought, or footless gale,

Now he is gone, thy dear one gone ?

My hope replies

With yearning eyes,

' A shadow with the lonely years increased,

A lengthening shadow pointing to the east.'

SPRING SADNESS.

O, IT is not for me the Spring returns,
And wakes the dust to live and bud and sing !
For some dear dust there is the lost heart mourns,
That knows no Spring.

O, it is not for me the bird athwart
The woodland dells pours forth her plaintful moan !
She loosens not the silence round my heart,
Sweet voices gone.

O, it is not for me the primrose blows,
Pale water-moons that gleam in dingles rare !
My bough nor bud, nor leaf, nor blossom shows,
My branch is bare.

O, it is not for me the cloud stoops low,
Freshening each little bud and leaf unseen !
These eyes have wept but barren showers of woe,
That make nought green.

O, it is not for me the morn from night's

Vast caves returns, the dark earth leaping o'er !

The light returns ; the Life, the Light of lights,

Returns no more.

For me the dim sweet eve, the cadent star,

The glow that points to some rich end, the balm,

That whispers inly of a rest afar,

An endless calm.

May 1868.

'Man fleeth as it were a shadow, and never continueth
in one stay.'

AH springs, ah Maytime sweet !

In whose wet prints, by copse and stream,

Blue violets like water gleam

    Beneath your flying feet ;

Ye snatch away my childhood brief,

While yet endures your opening leaf,'

    And with those white years strew your way,

        Ah well-a-day !

Like shed fruit blossom, fallen May.

Ah summers, summers fair !

That play about the naked thorn

With such sweet wooings, lo, one morn,

    The rose, the rose is there !

Ye snatch away my youth, my prime,
While with your rose 'tis yet Love's time,
  And all its burning loves decay,
    Ah well-a-day !
  Like rose-leaves trodden into clay.

  Ah autumns, autumns rare !
That with your dead gold stud once more
The fruited wall spring silvers o'er,
  And vales red plenty wear ;
Ye snatch away my riper years,
My fruit in thin thought disappears,
  While yet your lusty apples sway,
    Ah well-a-day !
  My ends like fallen fruit decay.

  Ah winters, winters cold !
Blue-hollowed in the setting sun,
Purpling your russet woodlands dun,
  Mute snows in silence fold ;
Ye snatch away my last grey days,

While yet your withered beech-leaf stays,
  Till by soft spinning night and day—
    So ends the lay—
The whole of me is whirled away.

EVENING CLOUDS.

Yᴇ evening clouds ! ye phantom heights !
That silently come out above our life,
And stand agaze with God across its strife,
Rosy and rapt with lovely dying lights—
   Ah sad, ah beauteous mountain shore,
      Once seen, then seen no more !

Had I thy wings, O evening wind,
Could but these palpitating mortal feet
Yon rosy crags and shining sun-slopes beat,
Deep in your azure hollows should I find
   Old loves, old faiths, old hopes of yore,
      Once seen, then seen no more ?

'And the star they saw in the east went before them.'

TO G——

I LOVE thee much as I might love a star,
  Thy day and night that makes thy purpose clear
Shine not within this world of mine, nor are
  Concentric with my swiftly-turning sphere.
        The storms that beat on thee,
Wake in my lightest aspen leaf no sigh,
  Nor shake thy steadfast shining light to me.
' I have no part in thee at all,' I cry,
  My solitary light that burns afar,
        My star.

The same Voice that informs thy shining way,
  Bade me come to Him on the bitter seas,
Where the dead faces stare up through the spray,
  With hollow mouths that drink the briny lees ;
        To toil without relief,

And clasp in mine cold shipwrecked hands forlorn,
  Where billows beat loud death against the reef,
Till all my woman's heart is rent and torn,
  When looking up I see thy light afar,
        My star.

Only when strength is spent, and faith burns low,
  And I am flung up on some barren shore,
And only hear an outer deep of woe
  Call to a moaning deep within ; no more
        May pierce the mystery,
Nor know that heaving waste of waters dark
  Still owns the sway of secret light on high ;
Nor looking up may any longer mark
  Thy jewelled lamp that shines no more afar,
        My star.

Ah then that dark despairing thing hath grace
  To draw thee from thy sphere of primal joys ;
Out of the fire is shaped a human face,
  Out of the splendour trembling comes a voice,
        Broken with man's deep pain,

And God's great pity, and as in a cloud
   I know thee there to lift me up again,
A Light incarnate into Love ; and bowed,
   I worship by thy side, no more afar,
       My star.

Ah sweet and melancholy love, so lone,
   So deep, so far, and sad as the last flight
Of solitary birds, when day is done,
   On their lone way across the dying light.
      Never to know thee more,
Never to touch thine inmost soul with mine !
   For when these faltering feet have reached the shore,
I shall behold thee fade in light divine,
   In dazzling depths of burning light afar,
       My star.

SONNETS

MEDUSA.

Gaze thou upon the face, serenely bright,
    Of Him whose countenance is as the sun
    Shining in midmost strength, ere yet is run
His race of fire.   Gaze, nor avert thy sight ;
Shrink not for any bitterness of light,
    Nor nightward fallings of thy soul, undone
    By heavenly lightnings till high use is won.
So when Life's Gorgon face, with dread affright,
Stoops close upon thy shuddering flesh, nor flee
    Thou must, but gaze, or fail in heavenward might,
Fronting unblenched the freezing mystery :
    Then that dear Splendour stamped upon thy sight,
May blur the deathful features, and for thee,
    Light-charmed, and safe, may smite them into night.

THE INFINITE WITHIN AND WITHOUT.

O THOU who hast the keys, thou hast o'erhead
  Unlocked an infinite of space unknown—
  No blue inverted bowl now shuts thee down—
Behind thy back an infinite, as dread,
Of time, and on the rubbish thou dost tread
  Of old dead worlds and age on age outgrown.
  The weight of two eternities of stone
Thou bear'st, the living standing 'mid the dead.
Guard thou the infinite within thy soul,
  For as deep sea-things can but breathe and be,
    By having that within which weighs without,
Else crushed by ponderous seas that o'er them roll ;
  So thou to live must breathe eternity,
    Or by dead Infinites have thy life crushed out.

THE INVULNERABLE LIFE.

THOU art immortal till thy work is done ;
  All things are under oath to harm thee not.
  The deep sea is not deep enough, I wot,
To drown thee, all the world too strait has grown
To give thee grave-room ; fire, that spareth none,
  In thy frail flesh hath neither part nor lot,
  Felt as moist whistling wind, not parching hot ;
Rude storms but waft thee to thy ends foreknown.
But when the appointed task is brought about,
    For which thy crescent moons knew bright increase,
    Then to the worms is cast thy life outworn;
The weakest moth may flap thy life-light out,
    The gnat may prick thee into nothingness,
      And shrill thy requiem on her slender horn.

ON THE UPPER GLACIER, GRINDELWALD.

I.

WHAT Titan agony has rent and torn
    Thine ice-bound frame, and on thy glittering brow
Stupendous furrows traced, thou Titan-born?
    While from thy riven heart that will not bow,
Thy frozen tears are poured in torrents still.
    What Hand thy stainless sapphire wrought of old
To these fantastic spires and turrets chill,
    And pinnacles that drink the moonlight cold,
And to thy feet thy crystal boulders hurled?
    Awe-struck I stand and gaze, eternal Love,
On the dread forces that have made the world,
    And like some Alpine harebell poised above
A roar of waters, trembling to their breath,
Yet drinking still fresh life from shuddering death.

II.

Nay, narrow Heart, more awful forces go
   To make the rain-drop on the wayside thorn,
Forces that lock and into union grow,
   With the loud shock of avalanches born.
Ah gentle Power ! that tam'st thy heavy hand
   To touch in benediction, not to crush,
Thy frailest creature, and, at thy command,
   Dread energies unharming round us rush ;
Bidding thy thunders poise a snowdrop's bell,
   And the wild force that rent this glacier, woo
The winged seed to falter in the dell ;
And lo, thy waters, wrought, when worlds were new,
With crash of deathful forces, mild as balm,
Lie trembling in an infant's shell-pink palm.

RAILWAY STEAM.

I.

Is this the power that has transformed the world?
This fainting thing the tenderest grassy blade
Can pierce, torn by each bramble in the glade ;
Or as it floats in thinnest wreaths uncurled,
Caught in the little aspen-palms empearled,
That chafe and fret it in their babbling shade
To nothing ; this that is, and is not, swayed
Lighter than thistle-down by light airs whirled ;
A momentary breath that scarce in May
The bedded gold can tarnish by the brook ;
That yet bound in by strong necessities,
Nor at its wayward will left free to stray,
The earth beneath its flying thunder shook,
And poured behind it streaming vales and skies.

LIBERTY AND NECESSITY.

II.

O THOU who hast shut in my living will
  With necessary laws on every side,
  Let me not deem in arbitrary pride
Thy purpose is in these to thwart me still,
Crushed into weakness that can nought fulfil ;
  Rather the everlasting Arms and wide,
  Leaning on which I mount, be these descried,
Too strong to break or bend to wayward ill ;
Resistances whose back-stroke is my power,
  Else dissipated in resistless air,
And left with free-will impotence for dower.
    Vast are the forces that oppose man's will ?
  So vast the liberty wherewith they square,
    Since of man's power they give the measure still.

BITTER SPRINGS.

I.

How bitter are the springs of human mirth !
 From him who, in his garret, with one hand,
 Shot his keen shafts of wit through all the land,
With her distraught, his best beloved on earth,
 Tied to the other with a silken band,
Nor while men laughed sun-struck beside their
   hearth
Knew his heart broke that gave those lightnings birth ;
 To him who shared the awful guiltless brand
Of her he loved ; and hand in hand they paced,
 Shedding mute tears, oft as the shadow came,
  That grim disfeatured all her gentle worth ;
Who yet with such delicious laughter graced
 Life's funeral meats, and lovely lambent flame
  From bitter whelming waves of woe flashed forth.

HUMAN SMILES.

II.

METHINKS but God and His good angels dare
   To look behind these smiles of ours, and see
   What ghastly shapes they hide of misery.
Does He so give us leave to use His fair
And blessed light? that in His azure air
   Hides with her smile no darker mystery
   Than lesser glories of the stars may be ;
Or skylarks hidden in her mid-day glare,
Themselves but darkened stars that palpitate
   In ecstasy of music strong and keen,
     In lieu of light. But when He lent, unasked,
His sunbeam to us in a smile, then straight
     Lost love, despair, rage, hate, are with it masked,
   And hearts behind it creep and break unseen.

ON DISTANT FIRING.

Is that indeed the deathful cannon's roar,
    Deep-mouth'd with discord, blood, fierce hate,
       despair?
    Scarcely it seems a ripple of blue air,
That breaks on yonder wind-loved aspens hoar,
Nor frets their lightest leaf to silver.   Hark !
    The breezy murmur of the hill-side bee,
    That makes her life one sweetness, distantly
Is heard across it.   Up aloft the lark
    Pierces in happy scorn that air-born wrong,
    With the keen silver arrows of her song ;
And with their thistle-down the hill-sides lone
    Confuse it, lightly tossed along the wind.
Great Mother, so let every jarring tone
    In thy wide lap of peace its requiem find.

Freshwater, 1874.

LOVE AND A WAVE.

SHE stood upon a sea-girt rock, my Love,
  All her fair form, that held her voiceless thought,
Poised silent as yon rosy cloud above
  The tumbling wastes of water tempest-fraught,
That in her bosom hides the evening star ;
  And round her beauty spread a mystery,
  Apocalyptic lightnings of the sea,
Voices and deep-mouth'd thunders from afar ;
Until she seemed, to love's fantastic fears,
  A thing apart from human uses, all
  Too exquisite for kiss, and touch, and call ;
    Till a great wave a moment veiled her charms,
And sent her beauty hung with sea-born tears,
    And thrilled with happy laughter, to my arms.

BOY AND GIRL.

I.

Two children on whose cheek the deathless rose
  Blooms in perpetual summer brave of hue ;
Whose rosy flower-palms clasp and close
  Like chilly clover-leaves in morning dew.
A boy and girl, who on each other look
  Intent, with the sweet steadfast glad surprise,
  With which in spring the first new-opened eyes
Look from their shining lids by copse and brook ;
Then sudden chase each other wild with glee,
  Or o'er some water-mirror bending bow,
And clasping, kiss, with sidelong glance to see
  If the two phantom children far below,
That glimmering mock them from the hollow blue,
Like them will meet and kiss each other too.

MAN AND MAID.

II.

A YOUTH, a maid, but on her cheeks the rose,
  That keeps no tryst with summer suns, but feeds
On Love alone, and with him comes and goes ;
  And wandering through the lonely meads,
Two hands that pendent shyly clasp to feel
  The mystic sunshine quiver through the frame,
  And eyes that meet not for delicious shame,
While round her, trembling, his embraces steal,
As a tall lily shakes when yellow bees
Are rifling all her sweets in golden ease ;
And words begun that break off falteringly,
  Like fruited boughs in summer winds asway,
That break with their own wealth ; and lips—ah me !
  That meeting, heaven and earth do pass away.

A PRAYERLESS SABBATH.

SCARCE have I breathed to Thee this day one word,
  And yet my heart held commune with Thee still.
Not a field-flower I stoop and gather, Lord,
  But with Thy gracious loveliness I fill
My empty hand.   And as the twilight breeze,
  Born in the fragrant dusk, with sudden gush,
Pours through the darkling heart of full-leaved trees
  The hidden moon, in golden showers and rush
Of lights, so all the rhythmic flow of thought
  That filled my soul revealed Thy hidden light,
And through my bosom scattered it unsought.
  The child walks sometimes silent, yet holds tight
His father's hand.   So, though no cry is cried,
Who walks in beauty walketh by Thy side.

GNOMIDIA

GNOMIDIA.

The Shadow feared of Man.

I.

Most men go witless to their graves like bears
Down a pole backwards, till all unawares
They fall therein ; nor once their stout heart dares
Turn round and face the leap that scares
  From the last wave-lapped step of life's dread stair,
  Into the unplumbed darkness, where, oh where ?

Man's Recusancy.

II.

The man who saw the whole world drowned,
No sooner safe on shore was found
Than lo, himself was drowned in wine.
Ah Lord, whereto Thy discipline ?

Man bales thy judgments out of mind,
And, to thy warnings madly blind,
Under Thy rosy arch of light,
Makes his own deluge in despite.

Laws made, Remake us not.

III.

Laws are but looking-glasses ; they
But show us as we are, nor may
Give us new shapes ; the crooked will
Left crooked still.

The White Cap.

IV.

Pleasures and wealth too oft like hangmen show ;
They hide men's faces with a covering,
So that their ends they see not as they go,
Then hang them in their feasts and chambering.

Whipping-tops.

V.

Be not, for shame, a top that only goes
   When it is whipped, then tumbles in the dirt,
     When sick, at prayers, at dice, unhurt ;
   A nine-days' saint that smacks but of the rod,
A swine that makes his litter of the rose,
   Flouting Beelzebub alike and God.

The Blood is the Life.

VI.

Yesterday's living sacrifice
   Is but to-day's dead carcase ; rise
Nor dare to offer the All-Living death,
   And dead decay ;
But fresh life-blood pour out, and warm new breath
   Each new to-day.

Who hath the Keys of Death and Hell

VII.

The grave is the dark keyhole of our life,
That holds within it locked the mystery
Wherewith our days are rife.
But we, alack ! have lost the key ;
And now we can but peep and pry
At the beyond, or bow our ear,
Some far-off harmony to hear.
And some do sigh,
' 'Tis utter dark,' and some, ' 'Tis glory,' cry,
Waiting till He who hath the keys comes by.

Fiat Justitia, Ruat Coelum.

VIII.

Quench hell, burn heaven, yet do the right ;
And though thou be but momentary dust,
Yet rise and set with stars in dust's despite,
With a wronged majesty of light,
Making thine ' ought,' concentric with their ' must.'

Dieu et mon Droit.

IX.

Thy rights?   Go to, thou hast but one—
To do thy duty, other none ;
Save some six feet of earth perchance to ask
To hold the refuse of thy finished task.

The Regency of the Will.

X.

The highest in thee is but weak
  While thou art here, thy rightful king,
But in his cradle.   Thou, bespeak
    Thy prayers, maidens whose vesture white
    Smells of the myrrh and cassia bright
Of those high fields from whence he came,
  To wait upon him.   Set thy will
  To guard his gate of life from ill ;
Call thy whole kingdom by his name,
Nor flam him off with half a claim ;
    Until he spring,
  Full-sceptred, and full-grown,
A majesty secure upon his throne.

Held in the Hand.

XI.

A jewelled goblet with a broken foot
Thou art, who canst but upright stand
When held within the Master's hand ;
    Else thou dost spill
    His light within thee still,
And his rich glories into dust transmute.

The Serpent-rod.

XII.

Thank Love Almighty for thy sins, O man !
Else thou might rot and die, till time outran,
    Hugging in peace thy hidden ill,
    And deep impurity of will.

But from thy breast glides forth this spotted snake,
Deep-eyed with hell, and dashed with fiery flake,
    A poisonous life from thy will won,
    That now without thy will lives on.

Not thee, ah, never thee, but ever thine ;
Ever it fronts thee loathing, fouls thy shrine,

Drugs with its poison all thy lust,

And smites thy manhood into dust.

Till mirrored in those myriad eyes of hell,

Thyself thou seest, thyself now known too well ;

    Abysmal depths of dark and light

    Sprung in thy bosom's infinite.

Fleeing thyself, thou find'st thyself for ever ;

The forces of thy being rush together,

    And knit into the spiritual will,

    No more caught in with chance and ill.

And that foul snake, but as Love's blossoming wand

Cast in the dust, thou know'st ; now in His hand

    A rod of wonders made, to smite

    Thy pathway over to the light.

The Master Carver.

XIII.

Not to make chips the Master takes His axe ;

From its keen lightnings think not thou to hide ;

    Nor will His arm relax,

    Till all thy wooden pride

Into the carven work He hews,

That lightly runs about His shrine,

And blossoms up about His feet divine

In lilies washed with sacramental dews.

The Children's Garden.

XIV.

God digs a ditch 'twixt day and day,

That so our feet not far may stray ;

Lets in bright inlets of death's sea,

Each four-and-twenty hours,

To shut us from our misery,

Breaking it small to match our powers ;

And of His bright eternity

Gives us but little plots of light,

Marked off by cool, deep trenches of the night,

Wherein fair flowers and healing herbs to raise ;

And makes a children's garden of our days.

Through Pain to Paradise.

XV.

Under the flaming sword alone,

That turns all ways to guard the gate,

Canst thou, O man ! pass back again
Into thy paradise foregone,
   And take again thy kingly state.
   Deep in thy heart as burning pain
It works, and shapes thee to high ends,
   And, hewing out God's thought in thee,
Lops the weak will that deathward bends ;
   Until, a sword of victory,
Slaked in thy life-blood, lo, it yields
Thee passage to the Immortal Fields.

Constancy to Truth.

XVI.

Follow not what the many teach,
Who cling like mussels each to each,
    Nor shape thy creed
    To suit their meed ;
Like the lone limpet to the rock,
Cleave thou to Truth, though all men mock.

Discourse not at Random.

XVII.

Who fitted is to mark thy words, first note ;
Pour not thy physic down a dead man's throat.

The Rose her own Evidence.

XVIII.

Do men abuse thee ?   Care not thou !
Rose-attar smells not less, I trow,
Of her own mother's bosom, in that men
    Do ' wormwood ' write upon the odorous flask.
Sweeten harsh labels with thy rose, and then
    No bitter name thy fragrant deeds can mask.

Strife.

XIX.

Who kindles strife a fire doth light,
    Whereat his enemies
Do warm their hands in his despite,
But keeps the smoke for his own eyes.

No Law, No Liberty.

XX.

Thou wouldst be free ; yet be not free
As dust and straws and feathers be,
   That eddy aimless in the air,
   Possessed and driven here and there.

Own a Divine necessity
Within thy human liberty,
   Then circling to thine inner law,
   A star's great orbit thou wilt draw.

The Saddest Tears.

XXI.

THE saddest tears not over cares
Are wept, but over answered prayers.

Obedience to Nature.

XXII.

Nature herself thou dost obey,
The weak, she rules, are ravened by the strong ;
Let preachers preach, and moralists prate of wrong,
Her instincts hold their constant sway.

Nay, man, thy nature is to be
Godlike, with attributes that regal show ;
A life of miracle within thee know,
That from all lower law sets free.

A life that gives thee Godlike power
To walk all deathful waters, storms to still
Of loudest passion, bid the palsied will
Rise up and claim her freedom's dower.

Thy mountain springs of being rise
Behind this phantom show of sky and earth ;
High possibilities in thee have birth—
The God within thee realise !

Be true to Nature's lofty plan ;
Cut not thy sceptre high from any hedge ;
The lower in thee to thy highest pledge,
    And make the beast still serve the man.

The Devil's Coin.

XXIII.

TAKE not the devil's coin, beware !
    He shows thee but Sin's smiling face,
The back of Sin he hides with care,
    Lest thou refuse his proffered grace.

Look not upon the crownèd face,
    That bids thee wanton in delight,
King it o'er God's restraining grace,
    And rebel reign in His despite.

Turn thou the golden bait right round,
    Look well upon the further side ;
The sin passed through, and thou discrowned,
    To death betrayed by life that lied.

No smiling face is now to see,
   A man, lo, with a dragon fights ;
A loathly hydra loosed by thee,
   Thy surfeit-maddened appetites.

Oh, well for thee if to thy hand
   Come some Ithuriel spear to slay ;
And bid thy writhen manhood stand,
   Scathed, but to beasts no more a prey.

Per Angusta ad Augusta.

XXIV.

' This wrong has ever been, this sin
Will last the world out,' do men cry ?
' Nature herself pleads a necessity.'

But thou, trust thou the law within ;
   By that supreme reality,
Dare thou to give all history the lie.

Yea, by that uncreated light,
   Whereof this solid earth and sky
Are but the fitful shadows cast on high :

Rise up and cry, supreme in right,
'This wrong is dead and damned to-day
Though through all ages it had held its sway !'

And broken though thine arm, thy spear
Nought but a bruisèd straw, yet smite
The ancient regent lie in all men's sight.

And though men flout at thee and jeer,
A gnat that buzzes up against a wall
Of rock in hopes to beat it to its fall ;

Though stronger grow the wrong each day,
And though beneath its iron feet
It pound thee small, and all thine ends defeat ;

Yet shall the world confused, astray,
Grow polar to thee, slowly taught,
And crystal out a Kosmos round thy thought.

Distiches.

XXV.

THE straightest bow must still be curved and bent,
That arrows swift in heavenward flight be sent.

The sap impeded in the noded shoot,
Is still the radiant birth of leaf and fruit.

The backward wave that climbs and falls in vain,
Still makes the onward strength of currents plain.

The forward motion balked and backward beat,
Is still the trembling birth of music sweet.

II.

Thy will must still be bent in storm and dark
From thine own ends, for God to hit His mark.

Thy springing hopes must still obstruction know,
For flower and fruit to crown the Master's brow.

The frustrate good that fools that life of thine,
May show the onward sweep of His design.

Thine upward, onward, still must know defeat,
For thee one note in His great psalm to beat.

Thy projects of a day must broken be
Into the plans of His eternity.

‘ Das Unglückliche Bewusstseyn.’

HEGEL.

XXVI.

DIVIDE, divide !
Be this thy philosophic pride,
Hold nothing fast ;
And if thy naked eye at last
Hold on to some unsevered whole,
Yet still press on to wisdom's goal,
And with the lenses' keener eye,
Shatter the crystal.   Decompose
Thy mother's tears, her dying sigh,
Into their atoms duly told ;
Phosphates that cabbage-stalks disclose,
Mucus and gases manifold ; [1]
Contract thy worship to a cell,
Then to a point invisible,

---

[1] ‘“Tiens,” dit-il, en voyant les pleurs de sa femme, “j'ai décomposé les larmes. Les larmes contiennent un peu de phosphate de chaux, de chlorure de sodium, du mucus, et de l'eau.” ’—BALZAC, *La Recherche de l'Absolu.*

Divide, divide !
Be this thy philosophic pride,
Hold nothing fast,
And thou wilt hit the truth at last—
When round the corner comes a thoughtless gust,
And man and matter vanish into dust.

THE MIND OF MAN.

O WONDROUS mind of man, that art not man,
But a strange medley wrought about his soul
By the enchantress Thought, who prisons him
Within the idols of her magic cave ;
Strange shapes and visitants beyond the will,
By which the holiest must stand betrayed.

O mind of man, that art all things by turn !
Lo, now a temple, where the young-eyed choirs
Do hymning make the silent vast of heaven
About us audible ; where light instinct
With heavenly meaning grows, and seeing God,
Adoring blushes into martyr's blood ;
And th' inarticulate deep heart of storms
Breaks golden-throated into gusty praise.

When suddenly a transept door bursts wide,
And lo, goat-footed satyrs chase, hot-breath'd,
A naked nymph, and the high arches fade
To boughs that pluck at her to have her down ;
And like to rent and flying leaves, the hymns
Are scattered wildly on the fading air.

And then the shadows shift and thou dost seem
A home, with children sleeping in their beds,
And shadowed lights and household talk subdued,
That, like the murmur of a settling bee,
Ceases a moment, then begins again.
When swift as thought an ambush fight bursts up
About the door, and groans of men are heard,
And the fierce struggle madly heaves and throbs,
And all the herby lea is trodden down,
And the mild daisy sets in blood.

       And then
Again thou risest to the inner eye,
A palace wrought with fretted gold and gems,
Wrung from abysmal deeps and stifling dark

Where magic mirrors, hung on every side,

Flash back dead yesterdays and sunken suns ;

And Time into a chisel beats his scythe,

And runs the purpose of the ages round

The marble frieze ; and master spirits store

Their life-blood from the world's great presses crushed,

The vintage by the Angel of the sun

Trodden, and stored about the oaken walls.

And the rich banquet glows with molten gems,

While the swift feet of dancers beat in time,

With claspèd hands and rhythmic motions sweet.

When noiselessly the tesselated floor

Splits like a cloud beneath the flying feet,

And lets the dungeon in upon the feast,

The clank of chains, blood-rusted torture wheels,

And tedious long-drawn yawnings of despair,

Shut in for ever on itself ; and all

The precious marbles sweat with dungeon dews,

The music dies in stricken sighs of men,

And hollow laughter hides a chill dismay.

And through the ever-shifting medley walks

The discoverable soul apart ;

An alien birth with a wronged majesty
That wraps the silence of the skies about it,
Like that disdainful hero 'mid the throng
Of twittering shades by name invoked in vain ;
Nor ever to keen philosophic doubt,
Nor tortured questionings of chemic art
Answers beside the mortal blood-filled trench,
Nor breaks her scornful silence through a life.

THE EARTH-SONG OF LOVE.

In paradise there danced and played
   A radiant child among the flowers ;
   But none of all the heavenly powers
His name could tell, his lips were dumb,
'Tell us thy name,' the angels prayed—
   He only looked and smiled.

In his blue eyes the morning woke,
   The asphodels that light they wear,
   Caught from the meteors of his hair ;
But like a star his thought was lost,
In the deep dawn that slowly broke
   Whene'er he looked and smiled.

They led him by the babbling river,
   They wooed him in the songful bowers,
   They bound his brow with deathless flowers,

'Sweeter thy voice than bird or river,
Wilt thou not speak to us for ever?'
  He only looked and smiled.

All things his radiant influence own,
  Shy birds with tender bills would sip
  The dew from off his blossom-lip,
The flowers for him had sweet home-looks,
The breezes sighed of him alone ;
  On all he looked and smiled.

In wrath at length the angels rose,
  His silence makes a want on high
  In all, and our hosannas die
Like faded palms upon his lips,
That ne'er in song nor praise unclose ;
  He only looked and smiled.

Then with a flaming sword of fire
  They drove him to a far-off world,
  A wandering star in darkness hurled,

A dim sad spot by some called Earth,
There to atone celestial ire ;
   He only weeping smiled.

But when men saw the radiant Child,
   They tore the flowers from off his brow,
   With cruel thorns they crown him now,
His heart they pierce, his infant palms ;
But now no more—mocked, pierced, defiled—
   He only looked and smiled.

For from his lips the iron band
   Was loosened, lo, a song he sang,
   A strange sweet song that heavenward rang,
While into roses burst the thorns,
A tongue no man could understand
   He sang, and singing, smiled.

He sang ; men met each other's eyes,
   With a strange sweet surprise, and smiled ;
   He sang ; the mother clasped her child,

' ''Tis bliss to suffer, Sweet, for thee,
And sweet the love that loving dies '—
 And still he sang and smiled.

He sang ; the son sought out his mother,
 ' Thy pangs have sweetened love to me,
 Let me but toil, dear Heart, for thee ; '
He sang ; 'Ah haste, Death comes apace,
We have but time to love, O brother '—
 Loud, loud he sang, and smiled.

He sang ; the lover clasped his bride,
 ' ''Twere ecstasy for thee to die ! '
 He sang ; and low she made reply,
' Love's shame makes sacrifice complete,
My maidenhood for thee, Love, died—
 Sweet, sweet, he sang and smiled.

And aged folk crept out to look
 On the new gladness of the earth,
 By little children's hands led forth ;

Dark guilt Love's bright occasion grew,
The dead a rapt expression took,
  As still he sang and smiled.

And loud he sang, and louder yet,
  Until that wild sweet song he sang
  From earth to highest heaven sprang,
And with angelic symphonies
That strange new cadence mingling met—
  And still he sang and smiled.

A richer diapason swells,
  In rapt surprise the angels gaze,
  New meaning gains the ancient praise,
In depths of light, a heart of pain,
To them Love's hidden nature tells,
  As still he sang and smiled.

And that wild star that lonely beat
  With death and sin the homeless blue,
  But for Love's broken home they knew,

Whence his deep fragrance through all space
Is poured, till all the worlds are sweet
   With love that suffering sings.

And still he sings that mystic song,
   That makes sad earth and heaven one—
   Sings, 'Love is sacrifice alone,
And God the love that ever dies,
That all may live immortal, strong,
   In love that, dying, sings.'

A THOUGHT FROM THE GERMAN.

Our earthly anchors, downward cast, we loose
    Through roaring glooms and gleaming deep-sea
        things,
    To grapple mid the ancient bitter springs,
With death and darkness in the primal ooze.

Hurtled by huge sea-monsters in their strife,
    Stared at by lidless eyes that never sleep,
    Grappling the slippery tangles of the deep,
The human hope holds hardly on to life.

But since in man we touch on mysteries
    That mock at sense and ever write it cross,
    Flashed o'er the limits of his earthly loss,
Made heir of God's great possibilities

The anchor of our heavenly hope, behold,
  We upward cast through depths of silent light,
  And tideless azure, up beyond the night,
Above the storm and blinding vapours' fold ;

Till grappling fast behind this veil of things,
  Within the windless haven it moors our life,
  Riding at ease through the wild tempest's strife,
Safe anchored still 'mid Love's eternal springs.

FROM THE PERSIAN.

THE gaunt-ribbed carcase of a homeless dog,
Cast by the wayside down, a lifeless log.

One spurned him with his staff where stark he lay,
One spat upon him ere he went his way.

Spake one : 'The rope about his neck behold ;
I trow they hanged him for a thief of old.'

Another : 'See how both his ears are torn ;
No fiercer brute to fight was ever born.'

A third, his garment muffling to his nose :
'Faugh ! living or dead, he smells not of the rose.

But from the crowd a mild voice passing, cries :
'No pearl the whiteness of his teeth outvies.'

Then all men in their spirit knew, who heard,
Jesus of Nazareth's must be that word.

For only He had love's divinity,
Even in a dead dog some good to see.

MAN'S GRATITUDE.

' I've heard of hearts unkind, kind deeds
  With coldness still returning ;
Alas ! the gratitude of man
  Has oftener left me mourning.'—*Wordsworth*.

GIVE but the gift that costs thee nought,

    And men will praise thee to thy face,

    And in their bosoms wear thy grace,

      And hold thee dear in thought ;

        And all the bough

Will burst in bud and blossom like a flame,

    Shaming thy meagre service with its glow,

And grateful lips make honey of thy name.

But give what costs thee bitterest gall,

    Enrich it with thy best laid low,

    Redden it with thy life-blood's glow,

      And round it with thine all ;

Ah, then beware

Lest our fond frail humanity thou trust :

The heavy-fruited bough, too weak to bear,

Will break, and bruising drop thee in the dust.

LOVE.

I.

Love the young-eyed, the beautiful,
Fell asleep in a bed of lotus flowers,
Rocked by the far-off currents cool,
    In the heat of the noontide hours.
But a water-snake gnawed at the root of the flowers
And the matted blossoms swept down with the
        stream,
The strong dark river that rushes with power,
        The fathomless river of life.
And Love awoke from his peaceful dream,
        And heard the dash and the strife
Of the waters, and caught the distant roar
Of the cataract freezing his balmy breath,
        And knew the thunders of death,
        And knew he would be no more.

And upstarting in agony vainly he sought

To stay the force of the tide ; but was caught

    In the deathful curves of the current,

        And hurried along

On the smooth dark swifts of the torrent ;

And up to the fatal brink sweeping,

    Heard the many-voiced song

    Of the dark-bosomed siren daughters,

And beheld the smooth swift plunge of the waters,

        And the dull

Vast mass of the foam in the shuddering shade

That would bury his sweetness for evermore.

    And he wept and he prayed,

Who had been so happy and heedless before,

And the vales were filled with the voice of his

      weeping,

    Love, the young-eyed, the beautiful.

II.

And, moved by his grief and his beauty, the waters,

    The deep dark waters,

The many-voiced deep-bosomed siren daughters,

Whose clear cool song it is death to hear,

Gave back the life that he craved to his prayer,·

But drew his soul after them evermore.

And he left the paths and the brooks and the
meadows,

Dewy and dappled with aspen shadows,

And trodden by sweet-breath'd kine ;

The homesteads and flowery pastures fled,

Where the long gold lights of the evening shine,

And all the wide placid life he forsook

Of the uplands in breezy silence outspread ;

And faded his feet from the sleepy hill-hollows,

Where the nested farms in the sunshine brood,

And one day another tranquilly follows,

And life and the brook

Flow on for ever the same ; and the glade

That knew him no more took a pensive shade,

And the wood pigeon sobbed of his loss in the wood.

III.

And lo, he became, ah fell compulsion ! became

The fair iridescent light without name,

That hovers and plays where the waters fall,
Where the deathful waters beckon and call,
The rainbow, the perilous splendour's breath,
On the shivering ·foam of the falls of death.

IV.

Ah, Love, and once thy young life was fair,
Beneficent on the primal earth,
That knew thee but as the morning's birth ;
But now in beauty, in storm, and despair,
A hovering splendour thou art from on high
   Where the turbulent waters fall for ever
      Of the dark ineffable river,
And but to behold thee is still to die

LOST IN LIFE.

My lost, my only Love, mine yet not mine,
Whom dear religious death took not, but life,
Hard life, not death who makes our loves divine,
 Setting them high
Like changeless stars above our changeful strife,
 That do not die.

I cannot bury my beloved Dead
Out of my sight ; I may not weep the while ;
To look on that dead face I dare not dread ;
 I meet thine eyes,
Across my breaking heart I chat and smile,
 My heart that dies.

My own dead kisses from those lips of thine
Thrill me with hopeless longings till I ache,
Lips where our spirits mingled, thine and mine,
O loved too well !
Lips that grown cold seek mine no more, yet spake
No fond farewell.

Thy hands where once I laid my wet cheek down
And found sweet ease of heart, now would not grasp
Me if I slipped and fell unhelped, alone ;
Hands folded now
From mine, that cold shake off my clinging clasp,
As boughs the snow.

I hear thy voice outside the closèd door,
Borne on my heart there comes a tender chime,
So sweet, so sad, so lost for evermore,
I bow my head,
And make my moan for love's most pleasant time
That now is dead.

And like some wretch, I listen to thy tones,
Who wounded hears cold waters babbling by,
Yet cannot crawl and drink, but parchèd moans ;
     While, as he lies,
That cool voice maddening mocks his agony,
     And fevered cries.

My thoughts that winged to thee their joyous way,
Now like poor birds whose mossy home's delight
All darkened strews the primrosed glades of May,
     Forlorn, alone,
Do beat the empty air in aimless flight,
     Their uses gone.

And that strong music, Love's own Orphic lute,
That bound my days in rhythmic dance, and slow,
Sweet, ordered motion, broken now and mute—
     No sequence keep
My unstrung days, my life confused falls low
     An aimless heap.

T

I sleep, and Sleep, Death's balmy brother—Sleep,
That knows not life, restores thee tender, kind ;
Thy lips meet mine, thine arms around me creep ;
  The day appears,
Those phantom kisses on my cheek I find
  In cold, cold tears.

And yet, my only Love, I blame thee not,
Since some impalpable influence alone
Has sundered us, I know not whence, nor what,
  Nor whither, yet ;
I only know life through lost love has grown
  One vast regret.

Like shipwrecked spars for self-same uses made,
We met 'mid seas by self-same tempests tossed,
Thy love a moment, by the same wave swayed,
  For mine implores ;
Then by some current swept apart and tossed
  On separate shores.

And yet perchance, as Sleep gives thee again
To this lost heart, so greater Death may move
To richer ends, and rend the veil of pain,
      The past fulfil ;
Till then, till then, my lost, my only Love,
      I love thee still.

THE WORLD-FORCES.

Forth rush the invisible tides of light, the ineffable
    splendour,

Giver and shaper of life, the shadow of Love, the
    Almighty

Energy primal, stupendous, which at the dawn of
    creation

Shook asunder the nebulous heart of the All, that
    swung into rhythm

Of worlds with their moons upon moons and belts of
    splendour concentric—

Rush forth as the snow-water leaps in spring from
    under the death-sheet,

And bounds down the crags in a rapture of torrent
    and jubilant laughter,

Bleaching the flat valley bottoms with boulders tossed
    down in its progress.

What world-crag shall bear the impact of light's irresistible forces,

The beat of her multitudinous pulses and surges of
sun-fire ?

What mortal sense can abide the refluent wave of her
glory,

Nor be caught in the swirl of its lightnings and.
dashed into uttermost darkness ?

But the strong tides broke on the heart of a new-
blown flower whose secret

The night had kept from the world and hid in her
odorous bosom,

And the refluent wave that ran back of the light's
irresistible forces,

And broke and flooded my soul, was no terror of
lightning,

But just a rose in her beauty, divine in her absolute
weakness.

CONSONANCES.

I.

My heart, my heart was like to sing,
So full it was of vague delight,
It could not speak,
And all my happy thoughts on wing
Went flying, flying forth to seek
Some sympathy of echoed light,
Some ecstasy of answering glow ;
And nothing found,
Above, around,
But three corn daisies in a row.

To my transfigured heart they shone
Just like Orion's winter belt.
I sought in vain
One warm June night, when one by one,
I counted o'er the starry train ;

And thought them gone, and wistful felt
That they but frozen fields must beat
In other skies ;
When, sweet surprise !
Behold, they blossomed at my feet.

And on their burning heads I spent
That gladness of a passing hour,
Until it grew
Half ecstasy, half daisy, blent
Inextricate in shape and hue,
A joy embodied in a flower.
All daisies now flash back afar
That passing joy
Nought can destroy,
And walk in glory like a star.

II.

My heart, my heart was like to break,
So full it was of anguish deep
It could not speak.

Only to ease the living ache
    Something it sought, some image weak
Of grief that may not wail or weep,
To speak what else it could not bear ;
        And nothing found,
        Above, around,
But one deep bed of bluebells there.

Down to the ground my face was bowed,
And thought was not, but only woe,
        As silently
Through shining mists of tears they crowd,
    Till all my vacant misery
Ran blue with them, in springtime glow
So fair, ah me ! so cruel fair,
        Why was my heart
        A bitter part
Of all that happy beauty there ?

And now no bluebell bed in spring,
But takes to me a touch forlorn,
        In gladdest moods ;

Nor may I see them glimmering
   Like water through the light spring woods ;
But lo, they seem one blue, blue morn,
When once I thought that Love had crowned
      Me, even me—
      O misery !
All dashed, and fallen to the ground.

NOTES.

NOTE 1, PAGE 23.

The ' Linus Songs ' were sung in the harvest-fields, or in the vineyards at vintage. They were of a tender and melancholy character, with a pathetic burthen, in which all joined, beating time with their feet ; and seem to have been inspired by some sort of unconscious sense of sadness over the golden corn laid low and the purpling grapes gathered and crushed. They derive their name from Linus, a beautiful boy brought up among the sheep-folds, and torn to death by wild dogs.

NOTE 2, PAGE 176.

The apparently fortuitous arrangement of leaves on the stem can in reality be expressed in fractions, of which the numerator indicates the number of turns of the spiral forming a cycle ; while the denominator expresses the number of leaves on that cycle, the cycle being the series of leaves included by the spiral line in passing from the first leaf to that which stands directly above it. Thus $\frac{1}{2}$ (grasses), $\frac{1}{3}$ (tulip, alder, birch), $\frac{2}{5}$ (leaves of apple, poplar, crab), $\frac{3}{8}$ (leaves of holly, plantain), $\frac{5}{13}$ (cones of *Pinus Strobus*), etc. It will be observed that each fraction has its numerator composed of the sum of the numerators of the two preceding fractions, and its denominators of the sum of its two preceding denominators, and it is found that all higher complications in normal conditions of stems exhibit some fraction indicative of the same ratio.

Spottiswoode & Co., Printers, New-street Square, London.

MESSRS. MACMILLAN & CO.'S PUBLICATIONS.

ENGLISH POETS. Selections, with Critical Introductions by various Writers, and a General Introduction by MATTHEW ARNOLD. Edited by T. H. WARD, M.A., 4 vols. Crown 8vo. 7s. 6d. each

Vol. I. CHAUCER to DONNE. | Vol. III. ADDISON to BLAKE.
II. BEN JONSON to DRYDEN. | IV. WORDSWORTH to SYDNEY DOBELL.

MATTHEW ARNOLD'S COMPLETE POETICAL WORKS. New Edition, with additional Poems. Two vols. Crown 8vo. 7s. 6d. each. Vol. I.—Early Poems, Narrative Poems, and Sonnets. Vol. II.—Lyric, Dramatic, and Elegiac Poems.

CHARLES KINGSLEY'S POEMS. Complete Collected Edition. Crown 8vo. 6s.

ARCHBISHOP TRENCH'S POEMS. Collected and arranged anew. Second Edition. Fcp. 8vo. 7s. 6d.

CLOUGH.—THE POEMS OF ARTHUR HUGH CLOUGH, sometime Fellow of Oriel College, Oxford. Eighth Edition, with new Memoir. Fcp. 8vo. 6s.

BY ALFRED AUSTIN.

SAVONAROLA: a Tragedy. Crown 8vo. 7s. 6d.

SOLILOQUIES IN SONG. Crown 8vo. 6s.

BY F. W. H. MYERS, M.A.

THE RENEWAL OF YOUTH, and other Poems. Crown 8vo. 7s. 6d.

ST. PAUL. A Poem. New Edition. Extra fcp. 8vo. 2s. 6d.

BY ERNEST MYERS.

THE PURITANS. A Poem. Extra fcp. 8vo. 2s. 6d.

PINDAR'S ODES. Translated, with Introduction and Notes. Crown 8vo. 5s.

POEMS. Extra fcp. 8vo. 4s. 6d.

THE DEFENCE OF ROME, and other Poems. Extra fcp. 8vo. 5s.

THIRTY YEARS. Being Poems New and Old. By the Author of 'John Halifax, Gentleman.' Crown 8vo. cloth gilt, 6s.

CHILDREN'S POETRY. By the Author of 'John Halifax, Gentleman.' Globe 8vo. 4s. 6d.

MACMILLAN & CO., LONDON.

www.ingramcontent.com/pod-product-compliance
Lightning Source LLC
Chambersburg PA
CBHW021038030726
47496CB00006B/1595